PETER RALPH

REVENGE
OF THE CEO

Typesetting and layout by WorkingType Design

Prologue

DOUGLAS ASPINE HAD SPENT eight years in Changi Prison for a crime he had not committed. Worse, he still had another seven years of the twenty-year sentence to serve before being eligible for parole. Yes, he had got away with many white-collar crimes, ruined the lives of thousands and had been, and still was a selfish, greedy bastard, but in his mind, that in no way warranted the injustice perpetrated on him. Framed! Framed for smuggling drugs into Singapore. Framed by a vicious bitch and her conniving brother because they blamed him for her spineless husband's suicide.

Aspine was fifty-six but looked many years older. He had been a big man, but now his ribs showed through his white prison t-shirt, he was bony, gaunt and the 70 kilograms he weighed seemed to hang from his 185-centimeter frame like a wrinkled shroud. His face was stark white, his forehead heavy with lines and his once perfect teeth were yellow and rotting. He had kept his hair which was shaved prison style, but whereas it had been jet-black only ten years ago, it was now white. Changi does that. There is the pretence of rehabilitation to the outside world, but prisoners know that once inside Changi, not even lip service is paid to it — Changi is a prison committed to punishment, and canings are frequent and meted out with brutal ferocity.

Aspine considered himself unlucky. Had he been incarcerated a little earlier he may have found a way to break out. The old Changi prison used by the Japanese in the Second World War had offered the possibility of escape but was replaced in 2004 by the modern, electronic, escape-proof new Changi prison. Aspine had racked his brain in a fruitless pursuit to find a way out of what was hell on earth.

The *keyless* Changi prison is broken into five rings, starting with small cells where prisoners wear tracking wristbands containing barcodes that they have to scan at strategically placed readers. In

1

many ways, this is an overkill as they are locked in their cells for a draconian twenty-three hours a day, every day of the year. The second ring is the housing unit where prisoners have medical checks and supposedly exercise, but there are no exercise or physical recreational activities — the twenty-three hours a day in the cell leaves no time for exercise. The prison laundry is in this unit and contains an X-Ray machine to detect inmates hiding in laundry baskets. It is under constant CCTV monitoring as are most of the cells. The third is the institution ring where prisoners and officers are screened and verified. The fourth is the cluster ring where visitors pass through a metal detector and have their possessions x-rayed and scanned for weapons and unauthorized objects like cigarettes, lighters, cell phones, and cameras. Two fences surround the cluster ring. The first has vibration detectors, taut wires, and anti-climb features. These are encircled by a network of video motion detectors. The cluster ring contains the Cluster Control Centre, the nerve center of the prison where all the security systems are integrated. The fifth ring is the complex ring and encompasses the main entrance to the prison. Visitors and prisoners use separate secure underground tunnels to get to face-to-face cubicles. Visitors have their thumbprints biometrically tested at the entrance to ensure that only those authorized have access to inmates. Observation towers outside the complex give guards armed with submachine guns optimum visibility. Aspine knew the security layout of the prison better than most of the guards and had long given up hope of attempting a breakout by himself. *He had not given up hope of getting out though, but knew he'd need the help of prison officers to have any chance of being successful.*

Aspine was blessed with rat cunning, and when the inevitability of jail became certain, he had taken out some insurance with the most powerful gang in Singapore. Most of the tiny cells housed four prisoners, but when Aspine was incarcerated, he was locked in a cell with only one other prisoner, Chin Kheng Hua, convicted lifer, murderer and gang member, who would serve as his bodyguard while he was imprisoned. The cell they shared was one of the few not monitored by cameras. Other than that, it was typical of a Changi cell. Tiny, with a hole in the wall serving as a small air vent. A squatting toilet bowl held a shower head that didn't spray but gushed in sporadic ten-second bursts. Inmates not only washed with this device, but it was also their source of drinking water. On his first day, Aspine was strip searched, and a guard screamed, "You are not a CEO in here, you are nothing. You shit, piss, bathe and eat in your cell. Think of it as home for the next twenty years." There were no fans or air conditioning. Computers, radios, televisions, and cameras were strictly forbidden, as were family photographs. Not that family photos worried Aspine. Sleeping arrangements consisted of a straw mat, a flimsy blanket, and a flimsier blanket that prisoners rolled up to make a pillow on the concrete floor. Recreational activities comprised three paperback books — hardcovers were not permitted, perhaps because prison authorities thought they could be made into weapons. The tooth-brush was made of soft rubber that could not be fashioned into a weapon, and clothes pegs were made of a brittle plastic that crumbled under minimal pressure. He had also been given a tube of toothpaste, a plastic drinking mug, a roll of toilet paper, a plastic spoon and a small towel. The clothing issued was a white t-shirt, black shorts, and shockingly uncomfortable plastic sandals. Aspine would have paid a fortune for a fan, but nothing that conspicuous would ever get through the five security rings.

There were no communal meals. Breakfast was four slices of white bread and a cup of vile, lukewarm, brown liquid. Lunch and dinner comprised overcooked cabbage, huge portions of rice and tiny pieces of fish or chicken. Inmates were also given one piece of fruit; apple, orange or banana on alternate days. The diet had minimal nutritional value.

Prisoners were expected to stand at attention in the presence of prison officials, but this was something Chin Kheng Hua never did, and Aspine copied him. The guards were wary of Chin and knew what his gang could do to their families if he was disrespected or mistreated. Clearly, he was the most powerful inmate, and other pris-oners avoided him in the hour each day that they had out of their cells. No prisoner would risk attacking Aspine and prison officials were courteous and respectful when dealing with him. For his part, he never regretted one cent of the quarterly insurance premium he paid to the gang by bank transfer.

Aspine had contemplated suicide but pulled back from the brink many times over the years. He smiled grimly recalling the times as a younger man when he had been told that hate would eat his insides out and destroy him. Hate was not a pointless and worthless emotion. Hate was the only thing keeping him alive in Changi – blind hate.

For the first time in eight years, Aspine saw a glimmer of hope. Lee Kim Wee was a young, deputy prison superintendent and Aspine had something that he was desperate for.

Chapter 1

SINCE THE DAY ASPINE was imprisoned he had been trying to find a contact that might enable him to see the outside world again. He had tried to befriend many guards and prison officials, all to no avail. His cell mate, Chin, told him that he was wasting his time, and that prison officers were rigorously screened. Besides, they would be extremely fearful of the retribution that the Singapore Government would unleash if they were found to have accepted a bribe. "Don't waste your time, old man," he said. Aspine resented being called *old man* but would agree, while never giving up hope.

It took months to get to know Lee Kim Wee. It started when Aspine stood to attention in his presence and touched his forehead in a form of salute. One day Lee said to him, "White-collar crime was very lucrative for you, wasn't it?"

"I was wrongly convicted for smuggling drugs. I was framed."

"Yes, that is what you claim, everyone in here claims they are innocent." Lee smiled. "But your local newspapers and articles on the internet claim you robbed your old employer of millions."

"I've never been convicted of a white-collar crime." Aspine grinned smugly.

"Mr. Douglas, all that proves is that you are a clever white-collar criminal. We'll talk again, soon."

It was 8 P.M., an hour before *lights out* when Lee entered the cell. Aspine was lying on his mat reading a paperback and got slowly to his feet. "Sorry, I can't offer you a chair, Mr. Lee."

"I wanted to see you by yourself, so I organized for your cellmate to have a medical check-up."

"Go on," Aspine said, leaning against the wall.

"My son has leukemia. He is only seven, far too young to be suffering in the way that he is."

"That is terrible. I feel for you," Aspine responded, false compassion written all over his face. *Oh, I know what you want. I've been praying for this day.* "I'm honored that you would share something so personal with me, but I am confused. Why?"

"The drugs that keep this dreadful cancer in remission are expensive," Lee said, looking at his feet. "They have a cure in the U.S., and if I can keep my son alive, the treatment will eventually be available here."

"What's your son's name?"

"Adrian."

"I'm not a doctor, and I have no medical contacts so I don't know how I can help poor Adrian," Aspine lied, wiping crocodile tears away.

"They say you have millions stashed away and I was wondering if–"

"Of course. I feel your pain, Mr. Lee, and I'll do anything and everything in my limited power to help you and Adrian. How much do you need?"

"Thank you, Mr. Douglas, thank you. If you can lend me fifty thousand, I will have enough for six months' supply of drugs. I will be indebted to you."

You sure will. "It's not that simple. You may face many questions if you're ever investigated, and there's a credit from a Cayman Islands bank in your account. I need a little time to move some cash to another account before transferring it to you."

"Thank you, but don't worry about me. I need the money desperately. My son is dying before my eyes." Lee sniffled. "When can you get it to me?"

It's getting better. He doesn't even want me to try and disguise the payment. "Do you have a laptop and dongle?"

"Yes."

"Bring them in tomorrow, together with your bank account details. I'll make the transfer, and it'll be in your account within twenty-four hours."

"You are a good man, Mr. Douglas."

You're a better man, Mr. Lee. You're my ticket out of here.

Aspine had not accessed his account with the Royal Bank of Toronto in the Caymans since his trial. He was pleasantly surprised to see that the balance of the account had grown to more than fifteen million and Lee's fifty thousand was insignificant.

In the weeks that followed, Lee occasionally smuggled soft drinks and chocolates into Aspine's cell, and let him have limited access to the laptop and dongle. Aspine knew where he was going and what he was going to do — he also knew that Lee would get him out –what he couldn't work out was how. He always knew Lee was going to visit whenever Chin was taken away from the cell.

One day when Lee entered the cell, he was distraught and didn't bother with pleasantries. "The drugs are no longer working, and Adrian is slipping away. They were holding the cancer at bay, however, now it is accelerating. I feel sick. What am I going to do?"

"Do you have any other children?"

"Yes, a daughter, Donita, who I love dearly but she could never replace Adrian, if that is what you're saying?" Lee replied tersely.

"Mr. Lee, you have mistaken my intentions. That is the last thing I would suggest. I only wondered how many in your family would need to travel."

"Travel?"

"Yes, to the U.S."

"You don't understand. The treatment costs half a million dollars and then there's the airfares, accommodation, and living expenses. I could never afford it," Lee said, wiping a tear from his cheek.

I just got lucky. Lee's predicament is manna from heaven. "Yes, you could. I'd pay two million to get out of here. That's enough to save your son and for you to start a new life somewhere else."

"No, no, I won't even think of it. No, it would bring terrible dishonor on my family and me. No, I will not help you."

"It may hurt your pride, Mr. Lee, but it's a chance to save your son's life. I know how much you love him, and you'll never forgive yourself if you don't take every opportunity God offers you. Think it over."

Lee flushed. "God? More like Satan. There's nothing to think about. I won't trouble you again."

Yes, you will, Mr. Lee. Your wife will insist you do. Don't leave it too long though, as time is running out for Adrian — and for me. Please hang on in there, Adrian. Please don't die before I'm free.

Chapter 2

A SPINE HAD A DOCTORATE in exploiting the misfortune of others and knew it would only be a matter of time, before Lee caved in. The first part of his plan about getting a prison official onside was complete, but he still hadn't worked out a way to escape.

Aspine had shared a cell with Chin since the day he'd been locked up, but despite this, he hardly knew him. He knew that Chin was dangerous, connected with the gangs and perpetually surly, but he needed help and had to tell someone what he had achieved.

"Congratulations. You fooled me, old man. You've got an official on the hook and a fairly senior one at that, but you have no idea how to use him. Even if you're lucky and get out of Changi you'll never make it out of Singapore," Chin said, through tightly compressed lips. "And when they catch you, they'll add ten years to your sentence and throw Lee in jail with you."

"Well, you seem to know everything. How do I get out?"

"You mean, how do we get out?"

"Hang on. I don't know if Lee will help you. I'm not going to ruin my chances by telling him that he's gotta help you too."

"You just don't get it, do you? You need Lee, but you need me more, and without me, you'll never get off this island."

Fuck, he's probably right. "All right, if it doesn't upset Lee you're in. Tell me what we're going to do."

"They hate letting inmates out of here for any reason but when someone gets violently ill or severely injured they take him to Changi General. He has to be near death though because they'd far rather use the prison's doctors and medical facilities. The security at the hospital will be tight but nothing like what it is here," Chin said. "I've got friends who can't get me out of here, but getting me out of hospital won't present them with any problems."

"Okay, I'm with that. We get out of here, and then we get out of the hospital. How do we get off the island?"

Chin grinned and rubbed his fingers together.

"How much?" Aspine begrudgingly asked.

"One million dollars."

"Fuck! What am I paying for?"

"My plan, my gang, the transport from the hospital to one of the marinas and the high-speed cabin cruiser and crew that will get us out of Singaporean waters and on our way to Thailand. We'll be in Pattaya in less than four days."

It's a plan, a good plan and Thailand is where I want to go. "How sure are you that we'll be taken to the hospital? How are we gonna fake the sickness or injury?"

"Lee will have to authorize it. Don't worry about how we're going to fake it. I'll take care of that when the time comes." Chin smirked.

The following morning Chin was carted off for yet another medical check, and five minutes later Lee entered the cell. His eyes were red and swollen, and it looked like he hadn't slept. "Adrian coughed up blood last night, and we had to rush him to the hospital. If he isn't treated in the U.S., he'll be dead within four months."

Fantastic, the chips are finally falling my way. "I cannot tell you how sorry I am. The poor kid."

"Please, spare me your false sympathy. We both know why you are offering to help. If I begged you for the money but said I would not help you escape, would you still let me have it?"

"Everything has a price, Mr. Lee, but you're wrong, I do feel for you and your son," Aspine lied. There was no point rubbing Lee's nose in it, and it may well tip him into making the wrong decision. "Let me tell you my plan."

Surprisingly Lee had no objection to Chin. Perhaps because he still hadn't made his mind up and Aspine could see him wavering. "How will my family get out? They'll be crucified if they stay in Singapore."

The tension in the little cell was overpowering, and Aspine sensed the answer to Lee's question would determine his fate. "I will pay one million dollars into your bank account as soon as I have your word that you will help. Your wife and children should fly to the U.S. post-haste where Adrian's treatment can commence immediately. I'll pay the other million just as soon as I'm in Thailand. How does that sound?"

"Yes, yes, I can live with that and going to jail to save Adrian is not a burden," Lee said.

Lee already knows too much about what I'm going to do in Thailand. What if he sings? He can't be left behind. "You're not going to jail. You're coming with us. When we get to Thailand, you can book a flight to Brazil, and your family can join you once Adrian is cured."

Lee looked relieved, almost pleased. "Why Brazil?"

"It's one of the few countries that's reluctant to extradite and refuses point blank to extradite its own citizens. That's why Ronnie Biggs fled there. It only takes a year to become a Brazilian citizen and Singapore's authorities will still be preparing the extradition documentation while you're swearing the oath." Aspine laughed. "And with more than a million dollars, you'll live like a king."

"I don't have any choice, do I? I'll do it, Mr. Douglas. I'm in."

I'm Mr. Douglas again. Phew, that was close. I hope this is not a double-cross where he blows me off for a million. If it is, I'll make damn sure the authorities are tipped off to look at his bank account. "Bring the laptop and dongle in tomorrow."

"I have them with me. I'll be back in five minutes."

Chapter 3

THE FOLLOWING MORNING SHORTLY after Aspine and Chin had finished breakfast, Lee appeared. "I wanted to see you both. We must firm up our plans starting with a date and time. Chin, Mr. Douglas informs me that you are organizing motor vehicles, and a cabin cruiser to take us to Thailand. How long will it take?"

"I had a visitor yesterday. It's already in play. There's no moon on Wednesday night in ten days' time. We will move fifteen minutes before lights out and, all going well, we'll be being rushed to Changi General by 9 P.M."

"Good. My family flies out to the U.S. tomorrow. There are those who might be suspicious about why my wife resigned her job so suddenly, and how she came to have the money to travel overseas. I have talked to some of my friends about the cost of Adrian's treatment, and they know I cannot afford it. The quicker we move, the better."

"Yes, yes. Raffles Marina is only nine kilometers from the hospital. The fastest speedboat in Asia will be waiting to take us to a cabin cruiser moored twenty kilometers out to sea. Once we are on it, we are free. Tell me about the security on the way to the hospital."

"You will be in the prison ambulance, and there will be two guards in the back with you. I'll be one of them. It is standard procedure to manacle and handcuff prisoners, but you will feign unconsciousness, and I will ensure that you are not restrained. There will be police cars at the front and rear of the ambulance, and there will be guards positioned outside the emergency department and the operating theaters."

"Is there anything else I need to know about hospital security?"

"The prison ward is on the fourth floor and prisoners are manacled to their beds. Security is tight, and if you are taken there, it will be impossible to escape. The police will want you admitted to this ward as soon as you get to the hospital, but I will insist that you need treatment in the emergency department. It's not going to be easy to get away."

"Let me worry about that." Chin grinned. "It will be far easier than you think."

A curtain of doubt came down over Lee's face. "I do not want anyone killed. I will pull out now if your plan is to kill police officers and guards."

"I told you not to worry; no one will be killed. It would be far too noisy. There is one important thing that you must remember to do — get rid of your cell phone at the hospital, or they will use it to track us."

"I'll need to talk to my wife in the U.S. How will I know how my son is? Can I buy a prepaid?"

"I don't trust the Americans," Chin growled. "It wouldn't surprise me if they tap her phone. You must not make contact with her until you are out of Thailand, and Skype would be a safer means of contact."

"How are we going to fake serious injuries? We haven't worked that out yet," Aspine asked.

"It's under control," Chin replied. "I will let you know in good time. However, the plan cannot go ahead without money. My colleagues need the million, and they need it now."

So, Chin is now our leader. Does he really know about Skype or is he just big-noting? A week ago, he wasn't even involved, and now he's calling the shots. How does that work? "I'll transfer five hundred thousand today and the balance when I set foot on dry land in Thailand. That'll give your friends an incentive to make sure I make it, and I won't have to worry about being scammed and left high and dry in Singapore."

"That was not our deal," Chin said, his upper lip turned up in an ugly sneer. "My people won't like it."

"Tough titties. They're getting a million bucks for a four-day cruise. If they don't like my payment terms, they can forget the deal." *As if I give a flying fuck what they like or don't like. They're not gonna walk away from an easy mil. No way. Who does this little fucker think he's talking to?*

13

Chin looked at Lee and spoke to him rapidly in Mandarin. Lee nodded before responding, and they both eyed Aspine off.

"Look, I don't know what the fuck you two are talking about, but the next time you talk that shit in front of me, the whole thing is off." *You fuckers. What I'm paying you upfront is more than enough. Make the most of it cause neither of you is going to be getting one cent more.*

Chin's face registered nothing, but his eyes were cruel and cold. Aspine could not hold his gaze. As he looked away, a shiver ran down his spine when he thought about the many murders Chin was reputed to have committed.

Chapter 4

WEDNESDAY CAME AROUND SURPRISINGLY quickly. The atmosphere in the cell had been tense, and Aspine regretted the way he had spoken to Chin. He had even offered up a half-apology that Chin had greeted with a thin smile, but his eyes had remained cold. Aspine had pumped him day after day about how they were going to fake their injuries, and now, with less than two hours to go, was stressed to breaking point. "It is nearly time, and you still haven't told me."

"Don't worry," Chin responded. "It's all under control, old man. Why don't you try and get some sleep? You're going to need all of your strength."

"Sleep? Are you mad? How can I sleep? Please, I'm begging you, tell me how we're going to fake our injuries?"

Chin put his hands behind his head and stretched out on his mat. "I'm going to grab a quick nap. Don't worry. Buddha has preordained our destinies, and we are in his hands."

Fuck, how can he sleep at a time like this? Aspine paced the small cell relentlessly, hoping that Chin would wake up and reveal some cunning plan. His face was relaxed, content, and the viciousness that it portrayed when he was awake had vanished. Aspine cursed, it was clear to him now. The two oriental fuckers had played him for a sucker and taken him for one and a half mil. He noisily washed his face, but Chin's eyes remained closed.

At 8:40 Chin woke up and looked around the cell. "It's time." He smiled, getting to his feet.

Aspine was beside himself with worry. "Please. How are w–"

Chin's fists struck repeatedly with blinding speed and brutal force. Aspine felt dreadful pain as his nose and cheekbones broke, and his eyebrows split. As he went down in a mess of blood, he could feel teeth rattling around in his mouth. Out of a bloody daze, he looked up, unable to move. Chin was screaming and smashing his face into the cell wall before he slumped to the floor next to the semiconscious Aspine. "I told you not to worry," he gasped, out of a blood-soaked mouth.

Lee was first into the cell followed by two guards and a prison doctor. "They must have fought and knocked each other out. They look terrible," Lee said, squatting down and taking Aspine's pulse. "He's in a bad way, and the other one doesn't look much better. We have to get them to the hospital."

"There's a lot of blood, but I'm not sure they need to be hospitalized," the doctor said. "I think we can treat them here."

"And if one of them dies and you have to face an inquiry, are you prepared to accept responsibility?"

The doctor paused and looked at them. "It's not my call, but I'm advising you that we can treat them here."

"So, you want me to accept responsibility for your decision," Lee snapped. "Well, I'm not prepared to do that. Guard, bring gurneys, notify the ambulance and advise the police. We're taking them to Changi General."

Chin and Aspine were placed in the back of the ambulance, and Lee, the prison doctor and an armed policeman got in after them. "Make sure they're manacled and handcuffed," the doctor said, addressing the policeman.

"No need, the hospital is only four minutes away, and they are both unconscious," Lee said, banging on the front panel and shouting at the driver to move.

"It's standard procedure and must be complied with," the doctor insisted.

"How dare you challenge my authority? My decision is made, and unlike you, I am prepared to accept responsibility for the decisions I make."

"I-I'm sorry," the doctor responded, "I've seen prisoners transported to the hospital many times before, but never without being secured."

"They're unconscious," Lee snapped, in frustration. "I'm sure this officer is not concerned."

"Not in the slightest," the policeman responded, resting his hand on the large gun sitting on his hip.

With sirens blaring the convoy pulled into the hospital's emergency department, where nurses were waiting with gurneys. Two minutes later, Chin and Aspine were wheeled into the hospital where they were surrounded by doctors. Four Buddhist monks dressed in long flowing red robes were hovering over another patient.

Chapter 5

THE DOCTORS MADE THE decision to operate and repair the men's facial bone damage, and Lee followed the nurses wheeling Aspine into an operating theater, while Chin was taken to the adjoining theater. Three policemen took up their positions giving them an unimpeded vision of the double doors to each theater. A few minutes later the Buddhist monks shuffled into the operating theaters without challenge from the policemen. Lee came out of the first operating theater where two monks had taken control and went into the theater that Chin was in. Chin and one of the monks were tying up the doctors and nurses while the other monk was covering them with a pistol. Lee left the theater and ambled over to the three policemen. "They've just started operating. They're under heavy anesthetic and will be out for at least two hours. Why don't you go and grab a coffee while you can?"

"You know we can't leave. Procedure states that prisoners are not to be left unattended under any circumstances."

"They're out like a light, and they won't be unattended. I'll be here, and I won't move until you return. Grab something to eat and get a coffee while you can. I'll cover for you for the next hour, but if you're running a few minutes late, don't worry. I won't move until you're back."

"We shouldn't, but I suppose if they're heavily anesthetized they're not going anywhere. Come on, boys, the food in the hospital canteen is not all that bad. Thanks, Superintendent, if I can ever do the same for you I will."

As soon as the police had gone, half a dozen male orderlies appeared wearing hospital attire. Lee entered the theater where Chin was and less than a minute later the orderlies wheeled a gurney out with a sheet drawn up over the face and body of an apparently deceased patient. A monk walked on either side looking sad and praying. The same process was being repeated in the adjoining theater, and a black hearse was waiting at the entrance to the hospital, and the bodies were quickly dispatched. The driver traveled only three kilometers to a darkened side street where he drove up a ramp and into the rear of a furniture trailer. "I felt you move," Chin said accusingly, "I thought you were going to give us away."

"I didn't," Lee responded defensively. "Those trolleys are designed for one person, not two."

"So, you'd rather I left you there."

"Knock it off you two," Aspine growled. "Where are we?"

"In the back of a furniture van, just in case our escape is detected early. The police will be looking for a black hearse, and it's hardly likely they'll look in here."

"How long until we get to the Marina?" Aspine asked. *The plan was perfect, and there were far more members of the gang involved than I anticipated. Chin is a lot smarter than I gave him credit for. The five hundred thousand was money well spent.*

"Not long, we're almost there. Another hour and we'll be on the cabin cruiser and in the clear."

Ten minutes later the speedboat was powering through the pitch-black night, and Aspine savored the salt water spray drenching his face. He put his hand up to wipe it away and felt the pain of the swelling and cuts. "Why didn't you tell me what you were going to do, Chin?" Aspine shouted, over the roar of the twin Mercury engines.

Chin laughed. "If I had told you, you would have fretted. The fear would've been too much for you. You may have even called the escape off. I couldn't run the risk, old man. Look at my face, I am in far worse shape than you, but I feel no pain, only the joy of being free. You would've never got out without me."

"Nor you, without me. You could've told me. I wouldn't have been scared," Aspine lied.

"Neither of you would've have escaped without me," Lee chimed in, looking miserable. "What have I done?"

"It's too late to worry about that." Chin laughed. "We're a team, and if any one of us had not been involved, then none of us would be here. Yes, a team. That is what we are."

Yeah, but I provided the money you little weasel. I was the key Aspine thought.

Thirty-five minutes had elapsed since their escape when they boarded the *Oriental Princess,* a souped up thirty-meter *Hatteras.* There was no moon, and the only sound was the cruiser's throbbing engines as it powered through a calm sea. The two escapees and the prison officer stood on the deck looking back at Singapore, each with their own thoughts.

"We did it," Chin yelled. "We did it."

Aspine tried to smile, but the pain was too much. "I'll never set foot in Changi again. What a relief to be out of that tiny cell. Eight years! Eight years of my life in hell because I was framed."

They were joined by an elderly Chinese man wearing seafaring attire. "Captain Goh, it is good to see you again," Chin said, ignoring the opportunity to introduce Aspine and Lee.

"The feeling is mutual, Mr. Chin," Captain Goh said, touching his forehead in deference to the gangster. "There is a stateroom for each of you fully equipped with toiletries and fresh clothes. We're doing thirty knots, but we'll drop back to cruising speed once we are well into the South China Sea."

"No," Aspine said. "Maintain maximum speed."

"Mr. Chin, we will not make Thailand at this speed without having to refuel. My instructions from your colleagues were that I was not to make any refueling stops."

"Don't listen to him, Captain," Chin said, looking at Aspine. "Traveling at high speed during the day will also draw attention to us. Continue as planned."

"I'm going to clean up and grab some sleep," Aspine said. *Fuck you, Chin. I'm going to enjoy stiffing you for five hundred thousand.*

"Me, too," Lee said, still looking morose.

Chapter 6

PANDENOMIUM HAD BROKEN OUT in Singapore when the three policemen had returned to the operating theaters after sixty-five minutes only to find that Lee had disappeared. Worse, they could hear muffled sounds, and when they entered the operating theaters, they found the doctors and nurses bound and gagged. Little did they realize that the escapees were more than sixty kilometers away en route to the Gulf of Thailand and Pattaya.

The policemen were immediately suspected and taken to Changi Police Station where they were subjected to fierce interrogation before being released and suspended from duty. It was only the evidence of the prison doctor that cleared the policemen and laid the blame firmly at the feet of rogue official, Lee Kim Wee. The Commissioner of Police hauled the Director of Prisons into his office and read him the riot act. This was more than an escape. It was a national embarrassment. All police leave was suspended, and the force was put on full alert embarking on a huge search to find the escapees. The black hearse could not be located, and none of the Buddhist churches had any knowledge of four monks attending Changi General, and the orderlies had disappeared without a trace.

Raj George, the billionaire Singapore businessman, was shocked. No one escaped from Singapore's prison system. He immediately called his sister, Jasmine, in Melbourne. She had mourned her deceased husband, Kerry, for what seemed an eternity after his suicide. She was stunningly beautiful, and men fell over themselves to ask her out, but she showed no interest, instead devoting her life to raising her two boys, Jack and Sam. Raj did not tell her that he had already organized for a highly respected Melbourne security company to watch over her. He knew what Aspine was capable of and that he would seek revenge on those who had framed him.

Fiona Jeczik, arch Aspine enemy, and Channel 16's head of news and current affairs silently cursed. The bastard was out. She compiled a short email and sent it to friends and associates who knew him, or may be impacted by his escape, saying among other things; *At least we don't have to worry about him returning to Australia as he will know about the Singapore-Australia Extradition Treaty.*

Aspine slept for nearly ten hours and was still lazing in a king-sized bed, enjoying the swell of the ocean, when he flicked the television on and caught the eight o'clock news. According to the newsreader, hundreds of plainclothes policemen had staked out Changi Airport after it was found that two passports in false names of the wanted men had been forged, and one-way bookings had been made on a 7:40 A.M. flight to Phnom Penh. It was speculated that Cambodia had been the fugitives' destination of choice because it did not have an extradition treaty with Singapore. When SilkAir 602 departed for Phnom Penh with no sign of the men it became clear that the police had been duped. The newsreader crossed to a furious Police Commissioner.

"Make no mistake," he ranted. "We will catch these criminals and return them to jail. Prison officials were deceived by a traitor within their ranks, and when we capture Lee Kim Wee, which we most certainly will, he will rue the day he was born. We believe he was the mastermind behind the escape after being bribed by notorious Australian drug dealer, Douglas Aspine. To be wronged or robbed is nothing unless you continue to remember it. Lee Kim Wee will find that we have long memories. Aspine only escaped the death penalty on a technicality, and perhaps our legislators need to close this loophole, so cockroaches like him, get to pay the proper price for their crimes rather than enjoy the relative comfort of our prisons. Chin Kheng Hua is a known gangster and killer. Citizens are warned not to approach these dangerous men but to phone 999 if they see them or suspect any abnormal activity. We are certain that they are still hiding in Singapore waiting for the heat to die down before they make another attempt to get out. I want to congratulate my men on thwarting the fugitives' plan to escape to Phnom Penh. I say to the escapees, 'Surrender, give yourselves up, and we will go a lot easier on you.' I repeat if you see these men phone 999." Photos of Aspine, Chin, and Lee slowly slid across the screen. *Fuck! I never realized Chin was that clever or perhaps it was his gangster mates. So, the police are laying most of the blame on Lee, and they would like to have hanged me. And what was that dopey prick talking about when he said, 'relative comfort of our prisons?' I'd like to see him spend a month in Changi.*

The latest *Sports Illustrated* was sitting on a set of drawers next to Aspine's bed. The girl on the front page was lithe, attractive, tanned and nearly naked. It was the first picture of a woman that he'd seen since before he was incarcerated. He knew there'd be more pictures inside the magazine, but he didn't immediately open it. Instead, he just stared at the cover– she was young, blonde and her red string bikini was tiny. He was pleased when he felt a stirring. *The bromide that I'm certain the prison authorities mixed with inmates' food, must be wearing off. I'm sure my libido will still be strong and fully functional, but climbing back in the saddle will be the only true test. Could there be a better place in all of Asia to test it than Pattaya?* There were more than a dozen pictures of the cover girl inside the magazine, and Aspine slowly savored each one.

The following day a small article appeared in *The Australian* headed 'Jail Break' and reported on the escape of convicted Australian drug dealer, Douglas Aspine.

Chapter 7

ASPINE SAT ON THE bow of the *Oriental Princess* admiring the beauty of the Gulf of Thailand. The water wasn't blue but a blend of shades that produced a color similar to, but deeper than aquamarine. It was day four, and he knew that before the dusk he would set foot on land as a free but wanted man. He had spent a lot of time on deck breathing in the pristine air, the swelling in his face had subsided to a light bruising, and he had a healthy tan. However, his once Grecian nose was twisted, broken in more than one place and still seeping blood. Chin and Lee had hardly spoken to him but had had many conversations among themselves that they abruptly terminated whenever he appeared. He had not met the captain, any of the crew or Chin's gangster friends. Not that he could complain, the food was ample, fresh and superbly prepared and it was only a severely shrunken stomach and a few broken teeth that stopped him from making a complete glutton of himself.

Chin sauntered across the deck, a cigarette hanging from the corner of his mouth. "We are rendezvousing with a Thai fishing schooner in about three hours. It is inconspicuous, and we will make land around 9 P.M. We'll be safe in Pattaya, but we don't want to draw attention to ourselves, and it would be silly to dock on a boat this grand."

Aspine had had doubts about the planning back in Singapore but it had proved flawless, and he wasn't about to disagree. "That was a nice little touch with the false passports and bookings to Phnom Penh. Was it your idea or did your bosses come up with it?"

"You saw it on the news? As it turned out, we didn't need the extra hours it bought. Nor did we need the van, but it never hurts to have insurance. The Thai fishing boat is also insurance. Whose idea it was, is unimportant, and I thought you knew, I don't have bosses just colleagues." Chin smirked.

"Was it your idea?"

"Why is it so important? It's the result that counts. Your problem, old man, is that you talk far too much. We shared a cell for eight years and I know everything there is to know about you, and here you are, as we are about to part, trying to find out about me. You told me far too much, and what you kept private, you told me at night when you were sleeping. You kept me awake many times in the first two years when you ranted and raved about those who crossed you."

"Is that why you haven't introduced me to the captain and crew?"

"No. There is no point. The more you know about them, the less secure they are if you're recaptured. Likewise, if they get into trouble, the less they know about us, the better."

"You're a very careful man."

"Yes."

"Then how come the police caught you?"

"I told one of my men to take out insurance by changing cars, but he chose to take the risk and not follow my instructions. The vehicle was tracked down, caught on CCTV, and my DNA and that of the deceased were detected."

"Does he still work for you?"

"He was killed in an accident while I was in prison."

"How?"

"He drove into a speeding bullet," Chin said through tightly sealed lips. "I have some organizing to do. There's a small leather bag under your bed if you want to take anything. You should grab a few bottles of water; you won't want to drink the water the schooner's crew drinks."

Was the speeding bullet comment a warning? Perhaps I better pay Chin. It will be my insurance, besides I'll still save a mil by not paying Lee, and what can he do? Nothing!

Aspine and Lee stood on the schooner's deck watching Chin shaking hands with the *Oriental Princess'* captain before boarding the fishing vessel with two of his men. It stunk, and Aspine went below deck only to be overpowered by the heat. It was nudging 100 degrees, and there was no air conditioning or luxuries on this boat. It chugged along barely making a ripple. "How long, Chin?" Aspine asked, sweat dripping off his face.

"About four hours. There's some shade in front of the wheelhouse. Why don't you sit there?"

"The deck's slimy and stinks."

"So, you'd rather be back in Changi?" Chin sneered.

"I'll be okay."

"Make sure you drink plenty of water. Stay hydrated."

"I can't believe you're concerned about me."

"I'm not. I just don't want you dropping dead before you've paid me."

Aspine found a small section in the front of the boat where he could get on the deck behind the bow. It wasn't dry, but the stench was bearable, and he stretched out. He wasn't able to snooze but could close his eyes, relax and make time evaporate as he had in Changi. It brought back memories of the floor in his cell, and he silently resolved to die, rather than ever go back to prison.

The full moon shone a golden pathway across the water and when Aspine finally stirred he looked over the bow rail, and the bright lights of Pattaya stared back, welcoming him. Four days ago, at this time, Chin had been belting the living daylights out of him, but it had been worth it. He found it hard to conceal his excitement, but when he looked at Chin and Lee, they were both poker-faced. What was wrong with them? Chin had been jubilant when they'd first boarded the *Oriental Princess* but now looked like he was carrying the weight of the world on his shoulders.

As the schooner pulled into the jetty, Aspine could no longer contain himself and shouted, "Yes. Yes." They had little in the way of baggage, and when they opened the jetty's self-locking cyclone wire gate, there were three golf buggies and drivers waiting for them. Aspine was no longer surprised by anything that Chin had organized, and a few minutes later the buggies pulled up next to a kombi van. The Thai driver helped them with their limited baggage before doing a U-turn and heading toward the bright lights. "Where are we going?" Aspine asked.

"My colleague, Chatri," Chin said, patting the driver on the shoulder, "has organized rooms for us at the Hilton."

Five minutes later they parked and caught the lift to the eighth floor. "Let me have the key to my room," Aspine said.

"First, we have some business to attend to," Chin said, inserting a plastic key into the door slot of room 812. The six men filed into the room. Chin headed straight to the laptop sitting on the bench next to a television. It was already connected to the internet, and the Google page was blinking. One of Chin's thugs took a chair and shoved Aspine into it.

"What is this?" Aspine asked as if he didn't know.

"You're going to pay five hundred and seventy-five thousand into this account," Chin said, thrusting a piece of paper in front of Aspine with the account details on it.

"I never agreed to pay you that," Aspine responded angrily. "That wasn't our deal."

"Mr. Lee, please explain how the amount was calculated. The old man doesn't seem to understand."

Chapter 8

"**M**R. DOUGLAS, I OWE MR. CHIN seventy-five thousand, and you owe me a million. Mr. Chin said you wouldn't object to adding it to the amount you owe him and deducting it from the amount you owe me."

"Okay, okay, but I don't want anyone staring over my shoulder while I make the transfer." *Fuck, I had no intention of paying you one cent more, Lee. I've already paid you far too much. Jesus, I can't think of a reason not to pay the seventy-five thousand to Chin though.*

"That's fine, but understand this, you're not leaving this hotel until my bank's confirmed receipt. My men will prop themselves in front of your room, and no, they won't be as silly as the police were at Changi General. You know why? Because I'll kill them if you get out without paying. And remember this, you have no passport, no documents and even if you do have contacts, they won't be able to help you. Without documents, you'll soon find yourself in a Thai jail."

One of the thugs stood guard at the door while the others went out on the balcony which overlooked the beach.

"It's done," Aspine shouted. "Give me the key to my room."

"Don't you want to know what the seventy-five thousand was for?"

"I don't really care. Give me my key."

"Tell him anyhow, Mr. Lee." Chin laughed.

"Mr. Chin charged me twenty-five-thousand for a passport, documents, a return economy booking to Rio de Janeiro and the promise that I would have no problem with Thai authorities at the airport."

"I did it for exactly what it cost me," Chin said, rubbing the thumb and fingers of his right hand together. "There were many palms to grease."

"He's not coming back, Chin. Why the return ticket?" Aspine asked.

"One-way flights by infrequent flyers are always suspicious, and the return booking is in–"

"Insurance," Aspine cut in. "Yeah, I know. What was the other fifty thousand for?"

"Do you remember getting annoyed when Lee and I were talking Mandarin in front of you?"

"Of course."

"Well, he asked me how much I would charge to collect the million that you owe him, and I said five percent. He asked me what guarantee I could give him. I told him that I would either get his money or I would kill you, and he accepted my proposition." Chin smirked. "So why don't you sit down and make the transfer?"

Fuck, fuck, fuck! These pricks are stitching me up. Worse, I actually paid Chin the fifty-thousand that is the price on my life.

"You didn't have to do that, Lee. I would've paid you," Aspine lied, staring at him accusingly. "I don't have that much in the account. I'll need to make some transfers from other accounts. It'll take time. I'm sorry."

Chin looked at Lee and burst out laughing. "Lee, didn't I tell you that is what he would say? You're a good liar, old man, but I know you better than you know yourself. Listen to me. It is Sunday night. You will make the transfer, and unless Mr. Lee's account is credited by Wednesday morning, I promise, I will kill you. It's nothing personal, just business."

"All right, I'll have to make a number of transfers. I just hope the banks respond quickly enough," Aspine said. "Go out on the balcony while I do them." There was only one transfer to do. After all, there was only one account.

"Don't hope, pray." Chin smirked.

Aspine felt ill as he watched the funds disappear from his account. The balance was down to a little over twelve million. "They're done," he shouted. "I'm going to my room."

"Not so fast," Chin said. "You might want to make one more transfer."

"Fuck that. I've paid everything I'm going to pay."

"Lee will be gone by Thursday and me, and my men will be gone by next Sunday. If you're still here, you'll be by yourself without a passport or documents. You might get lucky and find someone who can produce passable forgeries, but if you can't, I won't be around to protect or help you. For twenty-five thousand I can provide you with flawless documents and a passport. I will also let you have the contact details of one of Bangkok's most eminent plastic surgeons. He won't ask any questions and will put you in contact with those who can provide you with documentation after your appearance has been changed. You would be a fool not to accept my offer."

"You charged Lee twenty-five thousand and that included bribes and airfares. Why do I have to pay the same?"

"Because you can afford it." Lee smirked. "I could've asked a hundred thousand, and it still would've been a bargain. Without documents, you'll never get out of Thailand."

"Fuck you," Aspine said, turning around to face the laptop. "What choice do I have?"

Chapter 9

CHIN'S TWO THUGS EACH took a chair and followed Aspine to his room, where they sat in the corridor at the front of his door. He wasn't worried. He had made the transfers. Chin and Lee would have their confirmations tomorrow, or at the latest, the following day. There were no computers in the room, and Chin had said, "I don't want you to be tempted to try and cancel the transfers. As soon as the funds are received, you'll have a laptop."

What a way to spend my first night of freedom on land for eight years. If it wasn't for those two thugs, I'd be checking out Pattaya's bars and girlie clubs.

Aspine felt grimy from being on the schooner's deck, and the stink of fish was still in his nostrils. He flicked the shower on, closed his eyes and reveled in the hot water pounding on his head and body. Opening his eyes, he looked down at his body and was repulsed by what he saw. His ribs were visible, his hips poked out and his skin was loose and saggy. He cupped his penis in his hand and visualized the girl on the front cover of *Sports Illustrated,* but there was nothing, no movement, no response. *What have they done to me? Is it the bromide? Am I too old?* He got out of the shower, wrapped himself in a huge fluffy white towel, lathered his face and carefully shaved the stubble from his chin. His reflection in the mirror mocked and ridiculed him. He let the towel drop to the floor and stared — he was fifty-six but looked seventy, his face was heavily wrinkled, the volume in his lips had shrunken to two thin lines, his teeth were chipped and yellow, his once Grecian nose, now broken, was bony and far too large for his face, his hair was white, body emaciated, his skin sallow and his arms and legs were like shrunken sticks without any definition. His manhood was lifeless, and he wondered if it would ever rise again, and his scrotum, which was the only body part that had grown, was revoltingly oversized and saggy. He closed his eyes again, letting his mind drift back to how he had looked before he'd been framed at Changi Airport. Jet-black hair, perfectly capped teeth, a glowing complexion, full lips and a strapping muscular 100 kilograms. *They did this to me, and they will pay. I will make them wish they had never been born.*

Aspine picked up a sheet of the hotel's stationery and a pen and seated himself at the table in his room.

The first name he wrote down was Harry Denton, a director of Mercury Properties Ltd and its CEO before Aspine was appointed. Denton, as a non-executive director had undermined and ridiculed him from the day he was appointed CEO.

The next name was Fiona Jeczik, national television star. Night after night *the bitch* had accused him of being a cheating liar and held him up as a figure of derision on her shitty program, *Your Family Today*.

Then there was Mercury's former chairman, Sir Edwin Philby, who had sold him down the river at the first sign of trouble. Disloyal bastard!

Billionaire, Vic Garland, had cheated him in a land deal that had led to his demise at Mercury Properties.

Aspine hated all of them, but that hate faded into insignificance when compared with what he felt for Jasmine Bartlett and her brother, Raj George. They had unfairly blamed him for the suicide of Jasmine's husband, Kerry. The whore had held out the promise of seduction while planting drugs in his luggage, and her brother had tipped off the customs authorities at Changi Airport. They had framed him and made him endure eight years of a living hell. He had a special hate for them; he would leave them to the last and savor the thought of the pain that he was going to inflict. They had put him jail, but they had also kept him alive, because every time he contemplated suicide, he drew back, his throat dry with the thought that one day he would have his revenge.

Aspine buzzed room service and ordered a steak before taking a bottle of whiskey from the minibar. It took only two solid swigs to destroy it, and he opened another, pleased to see the mini bar was well stocked. He flicked the telly on and skimmed through *Fox's* channels looking for the Singapore news before settling on the BBC. Ten minutes later a toffee-nosed announcer said, "The two escapees from Changi Prison seem to have disappeared without a trace. Singaporean authorities claim they do not know if prison officer, Lim Kim Wee, is helping them or was taken hostage or killed. Police remain confident that they will recapture the escapees."

No, they fucking won't!

There was a knock at his door. "Room service."

When he opened it, with whiskey in hand, the two thugs hadn't moved. "Steak." He grinned, exaggeratedly breathing in the aroma. "Suck it up, boys."

Aspine would have liked to make a mess of the minibar, but after his fourth tiny bottle of whiskey he was bloated and couldn't drink anymore. *Fuckers. You not only destroyed my appearance you shut my innards down as well.* He knew he couldn't go out, so he propped himself up in bed watching movies until he finally lapsed into a fretful sleep. It was nearly midday when he woke to knocking and the sound of Chin's voice. He stumbled over to the door, pleased to see the thugs had gone. "The money came through. Here's a change of clothes," Chin said handing Aspine a small suitcase. "You need to make yourself presentable. I have a photographer coming in half an hour."

"Photographer?"

"For your passport and documentation. Think of a new name while you're getting ready. Something that won't draw unwanted attention and is easy to consistently sign. Come to my room when you're ready."

There were shirts, sports slacks, socks, shoes, sandals and even underwear. The shirts were a little too big, but everything else fit perfectly. It was yet another example of Chin's efficiency, and while Aspine had had his doubts it was now obvious, he was the head honcho of his gang.

Chapter 10

CHIN'S ROOM WAS BUZZING with activity, but the thugs were no longer present. A photographer was setting up a white screen and lighting while Lee was having his hair restyled, and a makeup artist was working on his face. The transformation was remarkable, and Aspine would not have recognized Lee had they walked past each other in the corridor. "How do you do that? He–he looks Chinese." Aspine asked the makeup artist.

She smiled, appreciative of the compliment. "You can do a lot with makeup if you know how."

"Incredible. I would've thought you'd need surgery to make changes like that."

"Not everyone can do it," Chin said. "She is the best in Thailand."

"Why Chinese?"

"China only introduced E-passports six months ago and the people who we use have a large supply of old Chinese passport paper and covers. Mr. Lee speaks Mandarin and is well versed in Chinese customs, so a pre-2012 Chinese passport is perfect. A Thai passport would've been easier, but he doesn't speak the language."

"Won't an unused passport create suspicions?"

"It might, but it won't be unused, there will be some departures and arrivals, including a visit to Thailand three months ago."

The makeup artist and hairdresser finished, and Lee sat down before the white screen while the photographer clicked away. Lee then signed a number of blank sheets of paper. "It is your turn now, old man," Chin said.

"What country's passport am I getting?"

"Australian. It will be more than satisfactory for banking and identification purposes in Thailand, but you should not attempt to use it for international travel. You won't be disadvantaged because you'll need new documentation after your surgery. What name did you choose?"

"Roger Cobram."

"You're so obvious; you had to include a snake as part of your name. An asp to a cobra." Chin laughed. "Don't do the same when you return to Australia. Don't drop hints and don't try and be smart for the sake of being smart."

Fuck. He was mute for eight years, and I now think he might be the only person I've met who's smarter than me.

"I may not go back to Australia."

"You will. The thought of avenging yourself is the only thing that kept you alive in Changi. Here, sign these papers, and we're finished."

"When do I get my passport?'

"Thursday at the same time as Mr. Lee. He's on an afternoon flight to Rio via Brunei. We'll have to make him up again in the morning before he leaves for Suvarnabhumi Airport. What do you have planned for the rest of the day?"

"Something light to eat. Then I might go for a walk around Pattaya and buy a prepaid cell phone. You'll have to let me have some of my cash back," Aspine said sarcastically.

"I wouldn't do that if I were you. Your photo's been on all the news channels, and someone may recognize you. I can get Chatri to buy you a cell phone."

"I don't understand, Chin. Singapore doesn't have an extradition treaty with Thailand. I thought that was why we came here."

"You have no idea how Asia works, do you? Everything revolves around money, and the Singaporeans have probably offered mercenaries like me, huge sums to bring you back. You've made fools out of them, and there is nothing they would not do to recover face. I know your courts would treat your recapture by mercenaries as an illegal arrest or extradition, but the courts in Singapore would have no such reservations. You'd be better off and far safer surfing the net and watching television in your room. Until you have the surgery, you should lie low."

How ironic. I'm free but still locked up.

Chapter 11

IT WAS THURSDAY, AND the makeup artist and hairdresser took a little over an hour to convert Lee to the photo that appeared on his passport. He was dressed in a traditional navy blue Chinese tunic suit and sandals. Aspine marveled at the simplicity of his disguise and could not imagine anyone challenging his apparent Chinese ethnicity. They shook hands, and Aspine knew he should wish him luck and say he hoped his son beats the cancer. *I can't. Yes, I offered you two million but never intended paying it, and you hired a killer to make sure you got paid. Fuck you. Why should I wish you good luck? If I knew it'd get me my money back, I'd tip the Thai authorities off to who you really are.*

"Good-bye, Lee."

"Good-bye." The little Singaporean man said, and then turned and followed Chatri out the door. It was a two-hour drive to Suvarnabhumi, and this was a flight Lee did not want to miss.

"You are a shallow man," Chin said. "He got you out of prison, and yet you couldn't bring yourself to thank him or wish him good luck."

"And it's my money that provided him with hope for the future. Did he thank me?" Aspine said defensively.

Chin laughed. "You would have liked to have double-crossed him and me if we'd given you the opportunity. I knew what you were like. Don't you understand? If you cheat everyone you deal with, you'll have no one to help you when you're desperate. Don't try it in Bangkok or you're likely to end up in a dark lane with your throat cut."

Aspine sat in his chair, surly and quiet, staring at the carpet. When he looked up, he asked, "What happens now?"

"I've decided to leave the hotel. Your room is paid until Sunday. You can take the laptop, and I'll give you two hundred thousand baht and let you have access to Chatri for the next two months. He is far

36

more than a driver. He was raised in Bangkok, knows it backwards and has many contacts. Do not upset him, as you need him far more than he needs you. He will take you to the plastic surgeon we use, and you should aim to get the surgery done next week. By the time Chatri leaves you, you should have healed. You'll no longer be recognizable and on your way to Australia. The surgeon will introduce you to those who can prepare a new passport for you. After you have it, burn all the documentation in the name of Roger Cobram. Leave no trace, because if you do, you'll leave a trail."

"I'll leave for Bangkok tomorrow. I agree, the faster I can get the surgery done, the better. I'll tell Chatri that I want to see the surgeon as quickly as possible."

"I've left two envelopes in your room. The first contains a list of Thai contacts and their names and numbers. It's only a backup in case something happens to Chatri, so hopefully, you won't need it."

"It's insurance." Aspine smirked. "What's in the second?"

"It has the names of some of my associates in Melbourne and Sydney. You may wish to avail yourself of their services. I've also left a number where you'll be able to contact me. Don't lose it."

"I won't need you again."

"Don't be so sure. You'd be stupid to run the risk of ever going back to Singapore. If you were fingerprinted, they'd throw you back in Changi or worse, perhaps hang you. Yet there is someone there who you hate, someone who framed you, someone you screamed about in your sleep night after night, someone who you'd like to hurt or perhaps kill. Mr. George is a very important person, and you're going to need help. I know what you have planned for him. You talked about it in your sleep, night after night."

I'll make sure that no one ever takes my fingerprints again.

"What did I say?"

"You yelled about planting heroin on him and the customs officials catching him in the same way they caught you. The ultimate revenge." Chin laughed. "Frame him in the same way he framed you."

"I savored it in my dreams," Aspine said. "I imagined sewing a quantity of heroin into the lining of one of his suits and tipping off customs officials in Melbourne the next time he visited his bitch of a sister."

"It's a good plan. It's simple and easily executed. Mr. George has more than ten servants, so access to his home would be easy if you knew the right people."

"You?"

"Exactly."

"But it would be expensive." Aspine grimaced.

"Yes, it would command a large price." Chin grinned. "One million dollars. Are you interested?"

"You know I am," Aspine said, extending his hand. "Thanks, we would've never made it without you."

"What a shame you couldn't bring yourself to thank Mr. Lee in the same way. I watched you trying to get close to prison officials for years while getting repeatedly knocked back. I never thought it'd happen and if you hadn't got to Mr. Lee, we'd still be in prison now. So, thank you. I'm glad I didn't have to kill you."

"Would you have?"

"In a blink. Good-bye, old man."

Chapter 12

A SPINE ENJOYED THE WARM sun beating through the windscreen as Chatri drove past some of Pattaya's many fine golf courses on the way to Bangkok. Palm trees and beautiful green foliage adorned both sides of the road. Young men riding motor scooters with their girlfriends sitting side saddle zoomed dangerously in and out of slower moving trucks and cars. Tourist-laden buses raced toward them on the way to the playground that was Pattaya. As they got closer to Bangkok, the traffic grew heavier, and the palm trees were replaced by factories and huge billboards advertising anything and everything from Rory McIlroy and Nike to the latest BMW. Chatri was thirtyish, unusually tall for a Thai, and lean and wiry. Aspine asked him to contact the plastic surgeon to organize an appointment and had been pleased when he had told them to come to his surgery as soon as they arrived in Bangkok.

Chatri pulled into an underground car park below a high-rise building on Silom Road in the Bank Rak business district. They entered one of a dozen elevators, and Chatri hit level 50. A few seconds later they alighted into a spacious foyer, furnished more like a palatial house than a surgery. The carpet was a plush white velvet and blended perfectly with bone suede couches and recliners with French polished walnut coffee tables sitting adjacent to them. The reception counter was a larger matching table, and a stunning Thai girl sat behind it with a small Commander Phone system on her left, a keyboard in front of her and the monitor to the right. It struck Aspine as strange that there were no patients in the waiting area and there was no signage on the walls. "Hello, Kannika. I have a patient to see Mr. Sonchai." Chatri smiled. "He is expecting him."

"Yes, I know," she said, returning Chatri's smile. "Mr. Cobram, please come this way."

Sonchai's expansive office adjoined the reception, and the décor was the same with the exception of his desk that looked like it had been carved from a huge piece of redwood. There was little on it except for a pen, pad and large computer screen. The wall behind the desk was covered by degrees, diplomas, and memberships of plastic surgeons' bodies. Large windows provided views of the business district and Silom road. Sonchai was small, tanned with heavily oiled black hair and wore a white open-necked shirt and gray slacks. "Mr. Cobram," he said, extending his hand. "Welcome to Bangkok."

Aspine was still getting used to Cobram, but this was not why he paused. The sound of the Thai sing-song language was unique but what he had just heard might well have come out of Manhattan. "Thank you. Are you American?"

"No, I studied at Harvard and then spent more than ten years at Mount Sinai Hospital's Plastic and Reconstructive Department in New York. I'm afraid I became Americanized."

Aspine could feel the surgeon scrutinizing him. "Your nose was broken quite recently. There is still some swelling," he said, "and your cheekbones were fractured too. We not only have changes but a little repair work as well. Tell me, what you would like me to do?"

"I want you to make me unrecognizable. I have a distinctive nose, a high forehead, and a protruding jaw, so at a minimum, they have to be changed, and I presume made smaller."

Sonchai came around from behind his desk and sat next to Aspine. "Look at me," he said, and then he ran his hands gently over Aspine's face. His fingers were surprisingly long and slender. "How old are you?"

"I recently turned fifty-seven."

"You've had a hard life. Your face is gaunt, and you look like you've lost an enormous amount of weight."

"Over thirty kilograms, and yes, the past few years were hard, but that's behind me now."

"I not only can make you unrecognizable, but I can also make you look far younger. Would you like that?"

"You want to do a facelift too?" Aspine frowned.

"The surgery is extensive, and the recovery will be painful. I can do exactly what you want and virtually leave you looking as old as what you do now. Alternatively, with a little extra work, I can have you looking a youthful forty-five. What would you prefer?"

Aspine laughed. "Doc, that's a no-brainer. Tell me what you're going to do — in layman's language."

"I will make an incision below the hairline and reduce the size of your forehead which will make it smaller and more youthful. The scar will be thin, and your hair will cover it. I'll remove the fat from your eyelids and the bags below them, this is a simple procedure, but the effect is amazing. I will need to completely reconstruct your nose. You've lost an enormous amount of weight from your face, so I will insert cheek implants to give you a fuller look. I will plump up your lips, and shave your jaw which is a minimally invasive procedure that will make it slightly smaller. Your ears are not pronounced but because we are altering the rest of your face, symmetry is vital, and I will make them smaller too. Finally, I will do a full-face lift with the stitches hidden behind your ears. It's a bit like the cut and polish your car gets from a panel beater after the repair work's been completed." He grinned. "Let me take some photos, and I'll show you before and after pics on my computer. What I show you will be very close to what you will look like after I'm finished, and you have healed."

"Sounds good. My teeth are terrible. I don't suppose you do teeth? I need crowns and implants."

"No, I don't, but I have a good friend who is one of Bangkok's finest periodontists. He will look after you. Is there anything else?"

"Quite a bit," Aspine responded. "I don't know whether you can do it or not but I need a scrotum trim."

"It's called a scrotum tuck, and it's not something I normally do, but it's a simple procedure, so for you, I'll make an exception. Let me see it."

Aspine stood up and dropped his pants while Sonchai knelt to get a better look. "Man, that's some turkey gobbler." He laughed. "Don't worry, by the time I'm finished it'll be as compact as what it was when you were a 16-year-old. What else?"

"Can you change my voice?" *I'd like to tell you what to do with your jokes, but then where would I go? Besides, I like the fact that you were trained in the U.S. and qualified to practice there.*

"It's actually known as a voice lift, and yes, I can. I can make the change quite distinct, but I cannot guarantee that you will not be croaky. Most of the time my patients have been fine."

"How do you do it?"

"I use a filler that I inject to plump up the cords and make them more limber. There are more sophisticated methods, but I've had good results with the filler. All going well, you'll have a youthful voice to match your new youthful appearance. There can't be anything else."

"There is. I was on the net, and I read that it's possible to change your fingerprints. I was wondering whether it's possible to do a transplant."

"And if it was possible, where would you get these fingertips?"

"There are seven thousand Thais killed every year on motor scooters in Bangkok. It should be the transplant capital of the world."

"That might be true," Sonchai said, shaking his head, "but we all have different immune systems, and unlike heart transplants, you can't pop a few pills each day and make them compatible. John Dillinger tried to do what you want to do, nearly a century ago. There have been cases of grafts from one hand to another, from the toes to the hands and from the stomach and buttocks. There is always scarring, and the intent is always obvious to the authorities."

"I don't care if there's scarring. I just want to destroy my existing prints. I even gave thought to having the tips amputated below the lower joints."

"How bad are you? What have you done? Are you a serial killer? I've never had anyone ask me to change their appearance, voice, and fingerprints. I do a lot of work for Mr. Chin, and I never ask questions, but you worry me. If it was possible you'd have probably asked me to change your DNA."

"Doc, I was wrongly convicted of drug smuggling. Yeah, I know every con says that, but I was. Anyhow, I'm on the run and need to get back to Australia. You're going to make me unrecognizable, and you're going to change my voice, but it will all be for nothing if I'm fingerprinted. I've never committed a violent act in my life," Aspine said, not counting hitting women and rape as violent acts. "And, Doc, no one has my DNA, so that's not a worry.

"I understand," Sonchai responded, "I can do what you ask but even with my skills, it will still be obvious and may lead to your detection."

Aspine paused. "What if my hands and lower arms were caught in a conveyor belt? They would be mangled and require extensive surgery."

"I'm sure you're not contemplating such a drastic solution."

"Of course not. However, when you were at Mount Sinai, I'm sure you had cases where patients had their hands crushed in factory or worksite accidents. Why can't you remove my fingerprints and match the scarring on my hands and lower arms to replicate an accident?"

"I've never had a request like that before, and it would be highly unethical if I were to perform such a procedure." Sonchai grinned. "However, everything has a price."

"Speaking of price?"

"I will require a bank check for twenty thousand U.S. dollars and another one hundred and thirty thousand in cash payable two days before the procedure."

"You're kidding. That's outrageous."

"It is, but what choice do you have? I have a scale of fees for patients like you with special needs. I know of no other surgeon who will perform all the procedures you're after, and even if you found someone, he would not have my skills. I am no lesser artist than *Michelangelo*, and my canvases are living, breathing, moving faces. Yes, my fees are a little on the high side, but you always pay a premium for the best."

"I'll get you the money on Monday. Can you operate on Wednesday?"

"Yes, but I'll only do one hand. You'll be totally incapacitated without the use of a hand. We'll do the other one in a few weeks' time."

"Where do you operate?"

"My operating theater adjoins my office. It is as sophisticated and modern as any in Bangkok. I have my own anesthetist, and my nurses have been with me for years. They have no idea who my patients are, and even if they did, they wouldn't breathe a word. There are two small suites on the other side of the operating theater for my patients to stay in while they recuperate. You will be here for three nights after

43

the procedure, there will be a nurse with you twenty-four hours a day, and I will be only two minutes away."

"You live in the building?"

"My apartment is next to my surgery. I lease the whole floor. Didn't you notice the double doors on the left as you got out of the elevator? That is the entrance to the foyer of my apartment. The views from that side of the building are to die for. Do you have any other questions?"

"No, until next week," Aspine said, shaking the surgeon's hand.

Chapter 13

ASPINE CHECKED INTO a suite in the Grand Hyatt while Chatri waited for him in the car park. Ten minutes later they were on their way to a branch of the Bangkok Bank where Aspine had no difficulty in opening an account. On the way back to the hotel he let Chatri know that he needed to go the bank and the surgery on Monday morning and that the operation was scheduled for 8 A.M. on Wednesday. Back in his room, Aspine flicked the laptop on and transferred half a million into his new account.

Aspine lay on the king-sized bed with his hands behind his head and reflected on the recent events. Nine days ago, he'd been lying in the same position, the difference being his bed had been a cold, concrete floor. After so many years in prison, the temptation to walk the streets of Bangkok was overwhelming, but Chin's words of warning cooled this urge. The desire to be with a woman had evaporated after he'd seen his reflection in the hotel in Pattaya. He was a vain man and what he had seen disgusted him. He removed his shirt and stood in front of the mirror and wondered whether he should ask Sonchai to remove the loose skin. He was a bag of bones and the decision to go to the hotel's gym, rather than go out, was easy.

Aspine was pleased to find he had the hotel's modern, well-equipped gym to himself. He broke out into a light jog on one of the treadmills before entering the weights area. He remembered warming up with forty-kilogram barbells in his younger days but was shocked when he picked them up. He tried to do some standing press-ups and nearly collapsed under the weight. It didn't take long for him to realize that trying to lift free weights was downright dangerous. He'd always thought that resistance machines were for females, but now he found them far easier than barbells. After doing three sets of lat pull-downs, he moved onto the bench press machine and managed two sets on light weights. He felt good using muscles that had atrophied while he'd be in prison. By the time he wandered back to his room he had tried every machine in the gym, and while he knew there was no noticeable physical change, the muscle soreness made him feel alive.

Aspine, having resolved not to run the risk of going out, conditioned himself to watch television, tracking down those he held responsible for ruining his life on the internet, and despite his aching muscles, working out in the gym and swimming every day until Sonchai operated. He didn't like being confined in the Hyatt but smiled thinking that it sure beat being confined in Changi. One extremely disappointing Google discovery was that property billionaire, Vic Garland, the man responsible for him being fired as CEO of Mercury Properties, had died. For many minutes Aspine stared at the screen, angry that he had been cheated of revenge and it briefly crossed his mind to pursue Garland's children.

What will that achieve? Garland's dead and will never experience the pain that he would have, had he been still alive. At least I totally discredited him before I was imprisoned and he would have died without out a vestige of honor. I'll just have to be happy with that.

Wednesday morning came around quickly, and Aspine was shown to the room in Sonchai's surgery where he would recover and told to remove all of his clothes and dress in a white gown given to him in a sealed plastic bag. A few minutes later the anesthetist introduced himself and gave Aspine an oral sedative and a tiny cup of water and told him to lie on the bed. It had an almost instant effect, and while still awake, he felt totally relaxed, almost trance-like. Two nurses entered the room and gently transferred him to a gurney covering him with a light mesh blanket. As they wheeled him into the operating theater, he smiled dopily at Sonchai, who was dressed in a blue gown, mask, and cap and standing next to a nurse in identical attire. They anesthetist put a drip into his arm and asked him to count to ten — by the time he reached six he was with the fairies.

Seven hours later Sonchai inserted his last stitch, and a few minutes later Aspine was wheeled into his recovery room and propped up in bed with pillows for support. His face was not bandaged. Nor was his scrotum but his left arm and hand were lightly dressed. He was on a drip, and a catheter had been inserted.

For two days, the nurses propped him up when he slumped over, acutely aware that he had to remain in an almost vertical position while his nose healed. Unlike most other surgeons, Sonchai kept his patients sedated on a light morphine drip because it minimized the risk of his handiwork being spoilt, and it made his patients far more comfortable than they otherwise would be. On the third day, he awoke — his throat was dry, his face felt tight and drawn, his groin hurt and there was a light throbbing in his arm — he was hurting and felt like shit. "Water, water," he said to the nurse in a raspy voice that he did not recognize. She filled a baby's cup with water and held it to his lips while he sipped from its small spout.

"You've been asleep for nearly three days. I'll get you something to eat," she said, pressing a buzzer by the side of his bed.

"I'm hurting. I need painkillers."

"I'm sorry, no more painkillers. The doctor says you have to get ready to go back to your hotel tomorrow."

"I'm not going anywhere in this condition. Get me a mirror," he rasped.

"Only the doctor can you give you a mirror," she said, as another nurse wheeled a small food trolley into the room. He hadn't been hungry, but the aroma was tantalizing, and a few minutes later the nurse was feeding him small spoonfuls of chicken broth. After he'd finished the soup, the nurse fed him some scrambled egg and for dessert, some mashed banana. He felt a little better and picked up a glass of orange juice and slowly sucked it through a straw.

"When do I get to see the doctor?"

"This afternoon. He will remove the catheter, and you'll be able to move around freely. The drip will come out in the morning before you go."

"Didn't you understand me?" Aspine momentarily scowled, before realizing it hurt. "I'm not going anywhere. I'm in pain. I'm not going back to the hotel like this."

The drugs might have worn off, but Aspine found himself drifting in and out of sleep. He wasn't a young man, and he had undergone major surgery. The voice of Sonchai woke him. "Wake up, wake up, Mr. Cobram."

He slowly opened his eyes. The pain in his groin had intensified. "Doc, I'm hurting; I need painkillers. Fuck, I'm drenched in sweat, and I think I'm going to puke. My throat's sore. My testicles are thudding and feel as big as tennis balls. You've gotta give me something."

"You don't need anything. You're coming along nicely. The operation went extremely well, and in a few days, I think you're going to be pleased."

"I want to see what I look like. I want a mirror," Aspine groaned. "Jeez, I'm sore."

"You'll be shocked by what you see," Sonchai said, nodding to the nurse. As she held the mirror in front of him, he let out an almighty *fuck*.

"Jesus, I look nothing like the images you showed me on your computer. I said I wanted to be unrecognizable, not look like Quasimodo. I can't go back to the hotel looking like this. Why's my voice so raspy? What fucking happened? No wonder I feel like shit."

Fuck! My eyes are nearly closed, my nose and forehead are both bigger, not smaller like the prick promised. I look like a toad with an elongated jaw. Mike Tyson couldn't have done this much damage. I sure am unrecognizable though. What has this fucker done to me?

"The swelling is at its worst, and you will see marked improvement each day from now on. If you'd prefer, you can stay here for three more nights. Your voice should lose its edge in the next few days but remember, I warned you that it could be raspy. I'll remove the drip and the catheter, and you can move around the room and the adjoining one. Don't just lay in bed because movement will help you. As I said, you're going to be very pleased with the result. Now let me have a look at your hand and arm," Sonchai said, unfurling the dressing to reveal swollen fingertips and stitches in the palm and hand. "Ah, it is perfect. I gave you the identical limb to a process worker who had his hands caught in a mechanized conveyor belt. The scars will not be deep, but they will reflect ragged, uneven cuts and support the damage sustained to your fingertips."

Aspine looked carefully at his hand and arm. He knew that the damage was minimal and yet it looked just like the pics of machine damaged arms he'd seen on the net. "Yeah, it looks good. When do the stitches come out?"

"In three days' time."

"And will my face look human then?"

"You'll notice a huge difference. Now let's have a look at your scrotum and those tennis balls. I'm sure they'll look beautiful." Sonchai laughed.

Chapter 14

SONCHAI HAD BEEN RIGHT, and as Aspine prepared to leave the surgery, he glanced in the mirror again. The swelling had subsided, but he found it eerie and unsettling when he saw his reflection and no longer recognized himself. There were no bandages or dressing on his face and only a light gauze on his arm. Surgery on his other arm was scheduled for two weeks. As he waited for Sonchai to perform one last facial examination, he mused. *He's a skilled surgeon all right but he'd be a lot better without the jokes, and a hundred and fifty thousand was fucking highway robbery.*

The door opened, and Sonchai bounded into the room with his nurse in tow. "Looking good, Mr. Cobram," he said, staring at Aspine's face while gently running his fingers from forehead to jaw. "Ninety-five percent of the swelling in your nose will be gone within eight weeks, and in six months there'll be no swelling. It will be smaller than what it is now and suit your face perfectly. Walking will help the healing process so you should get out during the day."

"I'm looking forward to it, and I intend to take in some of Bangkok's nightlife too."

"Ah, your voice has lost most of its edge. You sound far younger. You should be pleased. If you go out at night make sure that Chatri's with you. A blow to your face at this early stage could undo my artistry and be very painful. You need to be careful."

"Don't worry. I will be. Doc, you know, when you do my other arm I was wondering whether you might get rid of some of the loose skin around my stomach. It's hideous."

"Yes, it is something that is easily achieved. I will make an incision below the waist from hip to hip, remove the excess skin and tighten the abdominals. Recuperation time is around a month, and you won't be able to lift anything."

"It sounds like the scar will look worse than the loose skin," Aspine said thoughtfully.

"The scar will be fine and in time will fade. You will have a taut stomach, and there will be no comparison with how it looks now. If you like, I can do a full body lift. Buttocks, stomach, legs, arms and pecs."

"Just stomach. I can restore the rest by exercise and working out in the gym."

"As you wish. Bring twenty thousand in cash with you on the morning of the procedure."

"You're charging me? Christ, I've already paid you a hundred and fifty grand, and you want more!"

"That covered the specific surgery we agreed on. Abdominal surgery was not raised. If you were in a restaurant and ordered dessert as an afterthought do you think it would be free?" Sonchai laughed. "Anyhow it's up to you. That's my fee, take it or leave it."

"Fucking expensive dessert." Aspine scowled. "All right you win; you'll get your twenty. Now let me get out of here while I still have a few dollars left."

On the way back to the hotel, Aspine got Chatri to stop at a chemist where he bought a large floppy sun hat, a pair of sunglasses with oversized lenses and some factor 30 sunscreen. "Do you need me?" Chatri asked.

"Not today. Can you come tomorrow night? I want to have a look at the nightlife and Sonchai thinks I need a bodyguard."

"He's right. Is seven, okay?"

"Sure."

Aspine applied some sunscreen and took an elevator to the ground floor. A few minutes later he traipsed out the doors and onto Rajdamri Road. For the first time in over eight years, he felt totally free. Free to do what he wanted without having to look over his shoulder. He wanted to shout, "I'm free, I'm free!" Bangkok had the unique smell of food being cooked on the streets, and Aspine savored it. By the time he turned left into Rama Road, he was sweating heavily and strolling rather than striding. The sounds of heavy traffic, the continual beeping of horns and the buzz of motor scooters were music to his ears. The streets were busy with Thais going about their business and humming with activity. He wasn't going anywhere specific, but it was impossible to miss the Siam Paragon Shopping Centre. The air conditioning provided some respite, and blue-chip tenants like Jimmy Choo, Versace, Chanel, Rolex and Louis Vuitton attracted him. He bought three shirts and two pairs of sports slacks from Prada. By the time he got back to the hotel, he was spent but euphoric. He flopped on the bed and smiled. *I'm free at last.*

When Aspine woke, he could feel dampness in his underpants and when he checked his scrotum was weeping. *Maybe I overdid the walking. I'd better be careful until I'm fully healed.* He changed and went to the bathroom anxious to see what his face looked like. With the exception of his nose, the swelling had largely abated, and he was growing to like his new look. Sonchai had taken at least fifteen years off.

He set the laptop up and then ordered dinner from room service. He would find out everything he could about those who had ruined him, and by the time he boarded a plane for Australia, he would have foolproof plans, ensuring the demise of each of them.

Chapter 15

IT WAS PAST NIGHTFALL and Bangkok was bathed in artificial light as Chatri eased the van out of the car park and aimed it toward Aspine's desired location, the red light area of Pat Pong. The roads were crowded, and the footpaths were bustling with a pulsating energy.

"I'm not staying long," Aspine said. "I just want to experience some nightlife. We'll have a couple of drinks and then head back to the hotel."

"As you wish," Chatri replied. "You know there are cheaper places in Bangkok than the night market…for everything."

"I'm not buying, just looking."

"The bar girls will expect you to buy them drinks."

"I can live with that." Aspine laughed. "It's been a long time since I had a drink with a girl."

Chatri parked the van Thai style in a spot that was far too small by giving the car in front of him a few bumps and then doing the same with the one behind him. It was hot and humid, but Chatri was wearing a jacket and Aspine wondered whether it was because he was carrying a gun. He was standoffish and surly, and Aspine sensed that he really didn't like driving him around. *As if I give a fuck whether he likes me or not. He's getting paid for his time, and I'm the one who coughed up the big dollars to pay him.*

It was as if time had frozen the night market. It was exactly as Aspine remembered it when he had last been there more than ten years earlier. There was a police van at the top of the first lane for the protection of tourists and to ensure they weren't outrageously ripped off.

"Let's just walk the two lanes," Aspine said, pushing his way through the teeming masses before stopping to look at a stall selling imitation high-class watches and handbags. The vendor typed the price into a calculator and then handed it to a would-be-buyer who typed in a lesser price. This resulted in much head shaking by the Thai vendor who typed in a higher price. Aspine enjoyed the pantomime but knew it could be five minutes before a sale was consummated, so he moved on, stopping at the front of a bar in which there were more bikini clad girls than there were patrons. One of them in a revealing black bikini smiled and beckoned to him, but he shook his head and kept walking.

"Are you looking for a girl?" Chatri asked.

"No, I'm just enjoying the atmosphere," Aspine said, wiping perspiration from his forehead.

"Well, do you want to see a show?"

Aspine knew how rough the shows could be, and he briefly thought about it, but the heat, crowds, and confinement of the upstairs rooms did not appeal. "No, let's just do a circuit of the lanes," he said, picking up a Louis Vuitton branded leather belt.

"You're not looking for a boy, are you?" Chatri asked, without a trace of judgment.

"Hell no," Aspine laughed. "I'm no fucking faggott."

"Yet you don't want a girl and don't want to see a show. You're not like most *Farangs*."

Yes, I am, but what am I going to do with a weeping scrotum? Besides, my body looks old and disgusting.

Ten minutes later Aspine stopped in front of a bar where the girls were wearing white blouses, mini schoolgirl skirts, and stilettoes. "Let's have a drink in here," he said, ordering a whiskey as two of the girls approached him.

"You want to buy us a drink?" one of them asked.

Chatri responded in Thai, and the two girls went back to join the others.

"What did you say?"

"I told them to leave you alone."

"You did what?" Aspine snarled. "I don't mind buying them drinks, just so long as they don't try and sit on my lap. Get them back."

They were soon surrounded by young, happy girls and Aspine

ogled their nubile bodies and thought about what might have been. Chatri sat slightly away from them, sipping mineral water. "I don't understand," he said. "I know what westerners want when they come here. What do you want?"

"I know you can't understand, but I'm getting what I want," Aspine muttered, through tightly compressed lips. "I wanted to experience what was stolen from me. The good times, the girls, the drinks and my freedom. The only thing that kept me alive in prison was the thought of paying back the bastards who put me in there. A night like tonight just adds to the hate. They're going to pay, oh how they're going to pay. I've had enough, let's get back to the hotel."

Chapter 16

THE RECOVERY PHASE OF the stomach procedure was bloody and painful, but Aspine could not have been more pleased with the result. The loose skin was gone and replaced by a finely stitched incision below the waistline. Chin had been right, Sonchai was a surgical magician. As he recuperated he had scanned the net looking for pressure points that could kill, but that would leave no bruising or trace. He soon became convinced that they were a figment of the imagination of movie script writers.

He had better luck with timers, detonators and remote-controlled explosive devices. The amount of information was overwhelming, but with his engineering background, he had no difficulty comprehending it. HIV was something different. He knew that it could be contracted by needle but had no idea how long it took to appear after infection. It was perfect for what he had in mind. He spent days researching recreational drugs before narrowing them down to just one — ice. Finally, he Googled Chin's Melbourne and Sydney contacts — there was one in Melbourne and two in Sydney all of whom were described as *colorful personalities.*

Aspine would have preferred it had his hair and eyebrows been dyed black but instead opted for a medium brown. He looked and sounded nothing like his former self and could easily pass for forty-five, the age he would show on his passport and other supporting documentation. His only facial feature that hadn't changed was the color of his eyes, and they were so dark they could pass for black. He paid for two sets of documentation in different names including a Victorian driving license which in total set him back twenty thousand and confirmed what he already knew – Chin had ripped him off. His Australian passport in the name of Charles Adderley was supposedly issued in 2004 prior to the advent of E-passports while his Canadian passport was dated January 2009. He planned to be out of Australia before the Australian passport expired, but if he wasn't, he'd have the Canadian documentation as insurance.

Aspine's last appointment with Sonchai was brief, and the Americanized doctor did a final check of his surgery. "I am the Da Vinci of plastic surgery," he boasted, as he carefully checked Aspine's face. "Drop your pants."

"That part's fine, doc."

"Now is not the time to be modest."

Aspine reluctantly unbuttoned his pants. "Perfect, what a tight little scrotum, it could pass for that of a teenager. And the incision on your lower torso is healing beautifully. In six weeks, it'll just be a fine line. When are you leaving Bangkok?"

"I'm leaving at the weekend. Doc, I've been reading about pressure points and how martial arts artists and commandoes use them to kill."

"Yes, what's your question?"

"Can you kill someone by applying minimum force to a pressure point and do it without leaving a trace?"

"You've been watching too much television." Sonchai laughed. "Do you know what a full nelson is?"

"Of course."

"Well, you can kill someone by asphyxiation or by cutting off the spinal fluid to the brain using that hold. If executed properly there'd be no external trace, and without an autopsy, it might well pass for natural causes."

"That's interesting."

"You mean promising." Sonchai grinned. "But there's a downside. If the victim struggles and you have to apply more pressure, you'll break his neck."

"Were you the court jester in medical school?" Aspine snarled.

"Ah, Mr. Cobram, don't be angry and let me offer you a word of advice. I don't know what you have planned and nor do I want to know, but whatever it is, don't do it yourself, use pros who know what they're doing."

It was a hot and sultry Sunday afternoon when Chatri dropped Aspine at Suvarnabhumi Airport. They shook hands, and Aspine gave him all of the Thai currency that he still had in his wallet. The Thai was expressionless, and Aspine thought that he would kill you as soon as look at you. He had wanted to book first-class, but all of Chin's talk about insurance and being careful had played on his mind. If for some reason his cover was ever blown and his flights were checked, flying first-class would be a giveaway that it was him. It would have been clever to book economy because Douglas Aspine would never fly cattle class, but the thought of queuing with the plebs had been too much for him, and he'd opted for business. He had a small carry-on bag, the laptop, and eight thousand dollars. Only a few pages of his passport were stamped, and the last entry was in early 2005 when he had supposedly landed at Don Muang. He had extensive documentation indicating that he had been employed as an engineering consultant in Thailand and if any of his many references were checked, they would be confirmed. He cleared Thai immigration and customs without query, and five minutes later he was in the Qantas Club sipping a Jack Daniels.

QF24 departed at 6:25 P.M. arriving in Melbourne at 10 A.M. Aspine was concerned about the passport stampings, and the forgers had tried to convince him to travel on the passport of another country, but he had wanted an Australian passport. He knew that once he cleared immigration and customs, it would be far easier for him to open bank accounts and organize credit cards without being subject to questions about his background. Surprisingly there were a number of empty seats in business class, and he breathed a sigh of relief when he found that no one was sitting next to him. He had been dreading the small talk some travelers indulge in, but now he could relax with a Jack Daniels, his laptop and his plans.

The immigration official took what seemed to be an eternity to check Aspine's incoming passenger card and passport. "You've been away a long time, sir. What were you doing in Thailand for so long?"

"I'm an engineering consultant. I went up there on a three-year assignment, and somehow it stretched to nearly nine." Aspine laughed. "It's good to be home."

"You never wanted to visit?"

"My parents have passed away, and I have no siblings. There really wasn't a reason to return. Besides, I was immersed in my work."

"You're staying at the Hyatt."

"Only for as long as it takes me to find something less expensive and more permanent."

The official looked at the passport and at Aspine's face once more. "Welcome home, Mr. Adderley."

As Aspine sat in the cab on the way to the Hyatt, his groin and underarms were wet. He'd been certain that bloody prying immigration official had found something on his computer that wasn't kosher. *I'm home, and now it's time for revenge.*

Chapter 17

ASPINE WOKE TO A beautiful Melbourne morning and after a leisurely breakfast and reading the dailies he wandered the streets until he found an Apple store and bought an iPhone. On his return to the Hyatt, he booked a rental car and just before midday he was heading toward Armadale. Cars had changed a lot since he'd last driven but he had no problems and quickly inserted Harry Denton's address into the Satnav. Harry had been the CEO of Mercury Properties immediately prior to Aspine's appointment and had then become a non-executive director. He'd made no secret of the fact that he didn't like Aspine and thought his scruples and ways of doing business were unethical and dishonest. When Aspine had been stitched up by property developer, Vic Garland, costing Mercury fifty million dollars, Harry Denton had led the lynch mob. Later when Mercury's financial controller, Kerry Bartlett, committed suicide, Denton had vociferously blamed Aspine.

As Aspine drove along Toorak Road, he thought about Harry and his wife of nearly sixty years, Mary. He'd spent years dreaming of killing Harry and seeing the terror on his face before he met his maker, but on reflection, thought that was too quick, easy and painless. The research about pressure points had been all about murdering Harry who was now in his early eighties, so it would be no surprise if he were to die suddenly. *Harry, before I finish with the person nearest and dearest to you, you'll wish you were dead.*

Aspine parked the car two hundred meters from Harry's house and then casually strolled toward it. The house was old but well maintained, and its manicured lawns were surrounded by beds of roses of every color. Red and yellow flowering gums were complemented by glorious deep purple Bougainvillea's running along the side boundaries. As luck would have it, Harry and Mary were in the front garden admiring their roses that were in full bloom. The garage door was open, and Aspine could see a white Holden and a blue Corolla, the same cars they had driven before he went to prison. Harry was a wealthy man but not prone to wasting his money on cars. He was dressed in overalls and had a small spade in one hand and a pair of secateurs in the other.

"Beautiful day," Aspine said.

"That it is," Harry replied. He was older, but his face was full of character, and his piercing blue eyes had never aged.

"You have a stunning garden. A kaleidoscope of color."

"Thank you," Mary said. "My husband is a fine gardener." She was hunched over and frail and hadn't aged as well as Harry.

"He certainly is. Congratulations, sir, you have created a truly spectacular garden, and you should be very proud."

Harry couldn't understand it, but for some reason, his antennae were on full alert with this stranger. *Why is he wearing leather gloves when it's so warm?* he thought. "Thanks, you'll understand if I get back to my pruning."

"Of course. I'm looking for ideas for my garden. Do you mind if I take a few photos?"

Harry was about to say *no* when Mary said, "I'd love to see more gardens like ours. Please, take as many shots as you like."

By the time Aspine got back in the car, he had a dozen photos including four close-ups of Harry and Mary.

Mick McHugh was the Melbourne contact on Chin's list. He was a well-known underworld figure who liked to boast that he had a blemish-free record. Guilty of numerous crimes but convicted of none. He was also big into supporting charities, and his photo appeared regularly in the social pages of the Melbourne dailies. His associates didn't like his desire for publicity and called him the *plastic don* behind his back, a sarcastic reference to the infamous John Gotti.

It had taken two calls before McHugh returned Aspine's. "Do I know you, Mr. Adderley?"

"It's Charles, and no, but we have a mutual friend in Asia."

"Who might that be?"

"I'd rather not say over the phone. I need your help. Can we meet and then I'll tell you more? I'm probably paranoid, but it's just a little insurance."

McHugh laughed. "Insurance? Has our mutual friend just returned from an extended holiday?"

"Yes."

"Why don't you meet me in the bar of The Birmingham in Fitzroy at midday tomorrow? You can buy me a steak and a beer. I guess you know what I look like."

"Yeah, I'm looking at a pic of you on the net."

Aspine made one more call to a Melbourne estate agent who had a fully furnished two-bedroom apartment in St Kilda Road for lease and organized to inspect it later in the day. He would have far preferred to stay at the Hyatt but that was what those who knew Douglas Aspine would expect him to do, and while he wasn't worried, if something did go awry, he did not want to draw attention to himself. Chin's words of caution had impacted his psyche far more than he realized. He had instructed the Royal Bank of Canada in the Caymans to create a corporation in the United Kingdom and to open a bank account with HSBC that he could access. He would transfer funds from the Caymans into the HSBC account and then transfer them to the Australian account that he would establish in the next few days. Again, he wasn't worried, but funds transferred from the U.K. would naturally attract far less attention than those from an international tax haven like the Caymans.

As he had done many times since his escape, Aspine Googled Fiona Jeczik and got more than ten million results. She had done very well while he had rotted in jail, and was now not only Channel 16's star performer but sat on the board as well. He stared at her photos, her jet-black hair, fine features, olive skin, full lips and eyes as dark as his own. She had pursued him relentlessly night after night on her top rating television program, *Your Family Today, and* had attacked and pilloried him. He felt physically sick looking at her, and the pent-up rage tightened in his chest and welled up in his throat. He pushed the computer away and lay on the bed and stared at the ceiling. His original plan for the bitch had been to pay someone with no moral scruples to win her confidence and get close to her. Close enough to spike one of her drinks and then infect her with HIV via an addict's needle. The beauty of this plan was that it could take up to six months to be diagnosed and when it was, she would have no idea how she'd contracted it. *That's far too good for you. I want to humiliate you, to make you wish you'd never been born* he thought.

Chapter 18

MICK MCHUGH WAS WHAT Aspine had expected, a little brawnier than his photographs and a little older. He was mid-fifties, and while traces of his once red hair could still be seen, he was graying rapidly. There was a long scar running down the right-hand side of his face from his temple to his jawline, his forehead was wrinkled, and his jowls were heavy. He was sitting on a stool in the corner of the bar with two others when Aspine approached.

"Hello, Mick, I'm Charles Adderley."

McHugh did not immediately reply. Instead, he took a mouthful of beer and eyed Aspine carefully. "Take ya gloves off," he growled.

Aspine had got used to wearing black leather gloves to hide the severe scarring on his hands. He felt McHugh staring as he removed them. "Give me a look."

Aspine held out his hands, palms up. "Fuck, it's true you removed your fingerprints. When Chin told me, I thought he was bullshitting. Pull up a stool. I don't need you two," he said, addressing the men next to him, "I'll see you back at headquarters. What are you drinking, Charles?"

"Jack Daniels neat, thanks."

McHugh snapped his fingers, and a barman came running.

"Tell me what I can do to help ya."

Aspine's explanation was lengthy and covered all of the people that he saw as having crossed him and his plans for revenge. When he had finished McHugh studied him closely. "I don't think I've ever heard hate like that and I know of guys who've hated their wives and partners so badly that they paid huge money to have them hit. Yer worse, ya don't want to kill any of them; ya'd rather they suffer a living hell."

"I thought of killing them all right, and some days it was only that thought that kept me alive. After I escaped, I was devising ways how I could get rid of them. I even learned how to make remote-controlled bombs. Then it hit me, they're getting off too easy. You mightn't believe this, but if they'd hanged me in Singapore, it would've been a lot easier than the years I did in Changi. The bastards who framed me knew that, and they planted just enough heroin to ensure that I didn't get the death penalty. Do you have the resources to help me?"

"Charles, if ya have the money there is nothing that can't be arranged. Some of what ya want is novel but presents no difficulty. What you have planned for the old lady will cost you thirty thousand. Send her pics to this number," he said, handing Aspine a piece of paper. "It's a prepaid cell phone. Make sure ya buy one too and replace it regularly. Jeczik will be difficult, and the others will be a little tricky but providing ya have the money, I can provide the services. Speaking of money, I'll need one hundred and thirty thousand to get me started. When can ya get it to me?"

If only you knew, Mick. I am the king of using prepaid cell phones.

"It'll take three weeks. If I draw more than ten thousand cash a day, the bank will report it to Austrac and I don't want that."

"You don't have to worry about that crap. I'll give you the details of an account I have in Liechtenstein, and ya can transfer directly into it from wherever yer hiding your stash overseas. I try to make it easy for my clients."

"You have a Liechtenstein bank account?" Aspine grinned, shaking his head.

"What? Ya think they're confined to big shot businessmen like you? Get fucking real. I run an international business."

"Sorry, Mick."

"Yeah, yeah. Let's eat. The porterhouse here is great."

When Aspine got back to the Hyatt, he threw on a t-shirt and tracksuit and headed to the gym. He'd put on five kilograms since the escape, and while his body was still scrawny, the surgery and food had made a difference. His sexual urge was slowly returning, but he still had nagging doubts about whether he could perform. If it were not for this and his vanity, he would've visited one of Melbourne's many brothels. His favorite had been the Daily Planet, and he had spent many pleasant afternoons and evenings there — when the time was right he would again. On the weekend, he would move into the apartment that he had leased on the beautiful wide tree lined boulevard that was St Kilda Road. It was close to the city, superbly located and backed onto the Albert Park Lake and golf course. He felt good, the weights in the gym seemed lighter, and his endurance and muscle tone were starting to improve albeit from a low base. He missed his Grecian nose and the hawkishness of his old face, but he could not fault Sonchai's work. The face that stared back at him from the gym mirrors was youthful, handsome and relaxed — only the dark, brooding eyes of his former self remained.

Chapter 19

MARY DENTON REVERSED HER blue Corolla out of the driveway at 9 A.M. She silently cursed when she saw the fuel gauge was just below one-quarter knowing that she'd have to stop and fill up. The huge Chadstone shopping center was only seven kilometers away, but that was not the point. Mary liked to be prepared, and the gauge was far too close to empty for comfort. Fifteen minutes later she pulled into one of the shopping center's upper-level car parks and drove into a space next to a light pole and directly opposite the stairs, as she always did. A silver Audi followed her up the ramp. She liked shopping early before the shops got busy later in the day. She'd barely entered the mall when a hooded man got out of the Audi and within seconds was inside the Corolla. Strangely, all he did was move it, parking it in the same row next to another light pole that was a further twenty spaces away from the stairs. He climbed out thinking it was the easiest money he'd ever made.

When Mary left the mall overladen with shopping bags nearly ninety minutes later, the car park was full, but when she reached her space, a red Ford occupied it.

My God, someone has stolen my car.

She was shaken and fumbled in her handbag for her rarely used cell phone and called Harry to tell him what had happened. "I just filled it up, so it could be miles away by now."

"I'll come and get you, and then we'll report it to the police. Don't worry, it's insured."

"I'm not concerned about that. I love that little car. Don't you remember giving it to me when I turned sixty?"

"As if I'd forget." Harry laughed. "I'll be there in ten minutes. Don't stress."

That evening the local police called, and when Harry answered, he was told Mary's car had been found in the car park. "I think your wife might've have forgotten where she parked, sir. It happens you know. We haven't moved it, and the car park is nearly empty now, so you can't miss it."

"Yes, yes, I understand. We'll come down now."

When Harry told Mary what the policeman had said, she was furious. "I know where I parked. I'm not senile, and I'm not suffering dementia. How dare he say that."

There were only a few cars left in the car park, and Harry pulled up next to Mary's Corolla. "I better make sure everything's okay before you drive it, darling. Let me have the keys."

He quickly glanced through the windows and saw nothing untoward before climbing behind the steering wheel and starting the engine. His eyes focused on the fuel gauge as the needle slowly went from empty to full. No one had driven the car, and the likelihood was that Mary had simply forgotten where she parked.

"Is it all right?" Mary asked.

"It's fine. I'll follow you home just in case there's something I've missed."

The following day Mary received a call from the police asking her and Harry to could come down to Murrumbeena police station. As Harry drove out of his street, a United Energy van that had been parked in front of the house pulled up in the driveway. The house was old with no deadlocks or security cameras. The man and woman in the van were soon in the house. The man hid eight thousand dollars in cash in the back of the freezer and bugged the phone handsets and the kitchen. The woman diligently rifled through documents until she found what she was looking for. Within five minutes they were reversing out of the driveway.

"You heard the phone ring," Mary snapped, as Harry drove slowly away from the police station. "The police said they wanted to talk to us about my car."

"Funny, no one at the station knew about it."

"What's that mean? I did get the call. I did!"

"Are you sure the call wasn't from Oakleigh police station?"

"Yes, I'm sure. Stop talking to me like I'm a five-year-old."

Mick McHugh's associates had planted the bug in the kitchen so that recorded conversations could be given to Aspine so he could monitor his plan. With the bugs installed in the phones, they would know Harry's and Mary's movements without having to wait out on the street for them to go out.

Two days later and not long after Harry had gone out a uniformed Multinet Gas maintenance man knocked on the Dentons' door and told Mary that he was performing a routine maintenance check on the meter. She asked him if he would like a cup of coffee or tea, but he declined, saying that he was on a tight deadline. A few minutes later he knocked on the door with a large pad in his hand. "Can I get your signature? It just acknowledges that I checked your meter and proves to my bosses that I was here." He laughed. "I have more than thirty meters to check and so little time to do it."

"Certainly," Mary said, taking a pen from him and signing the bottom of the form where he was pointing.

Sir Edwin Philby had no idea he was being followed. Why would he? Prior to the near collapse of Mercury Properties Limited, a company of which he had been chairman, he was a significant figure in the Melbourne establishment. After the debacle, he was blamed for appointing Douglas Aspine as the company's CEO and lost more than ten directorships of major Australian and international companies. He'd also lost powerful political connections who now refused to take his calls or acknowledge him. Yes, he had been important, but that was before Douglas Aspine had entered his life. The board might have sacked Aspine but the damage had already been done, and the business community was unforgiving. Now Philby's only remaining claim to power was as chairman of a charitable trust created to give away his late father's vast wealth. He parked his Jaguar, put his notebook-tablet under his arm and strode across Collins Street toward his office.

Chapter 20

PHILBY'S TOORAK MANSION WAS surrounded by a high brick fence. Security lights and cameras were affixed just below the roof line. Street lights cast long shadows along the street and hid the black sedan in which two men were engaged in animated discussion.

"Look at the security system. How are we going to get in?"

The other man laughed. "It's ancient. I doubt it even works. If it does, it'll only take a few minutes to deactivate. How long will you need with the computers?"

"Thirty minutes max."

"Have ya ever had a job like this before? I mean what type of sick fuck plants kiddie porn on someone else's computers?"

"Never. Dunno, the boss also gave me a couple of hundred pics to hide in the poor prick's study. I wonder what he did to the sicko who's out to get him."

"Ya know he's a knight, don't you? Sir Edwin Philby."

"He won't be after this. Does it worry you?"

"Nah, it'll be the easiest ten grand I've ever picked up."

"So, when do we move?"

"The boss is gonna organize for him to get called away this Friday night. We'll do it then."

"Doesn't anyone else live here? Christ, the place is bloody gigantic."

"He's got a live-in cook, but he's off on Friday night, and he always goes to the football. I wish every job was this easy."

Ten minutes after Harry and Mary Denton left to go to a charity fund-raiser, a large truck pulled into their driveway, and three men wearing khaki overalls got out. Soon they were clearing one of Harry's prized rose beds and digging up the pavers that formed the driveway. The pavers had been laid on a thick base of concrete and did not come away easily, but the men toiled hard and soon had more than half removed. The boss told his men to keep going while he took a jackhammer from the back of the truck and started breaking up the concrete. He'd just started when a white Holden stopped in the street, and a furious Harry Denton jumped out and charged up the driveway.

"What are you doing? What are you doing?" He shouted. "What have you done to my roses? No, no, no!"

"Settle down. We're putting in a new brick driveway and a small hardstanding area where the rose bed was."

"You fool. You've got the wrong house. We don't want a new driveway."

Mary hadn't been as fast as Harry, but now she was next to him.

"Hello, Mrs. Denton." The man smiled. "Can you please set your husband straight?"

"Do I know you?"

"What is this? You order a new driveway, and now you can't remember me?"

"You're mistaken. I've never set eyes on you before today," Mary snapped.

"Show me the paperwork," Harry growled. "Then you'll realize you've got the wrong property and the wrong woman."

The man rifled around in his overalls before producing a printed contract for a new driveway and hardstanding area for ten thousand dollars. At the bottom of the form above the printed word *acceptance* was Mary's unmistakable signature, and a receipt for a deposit of two thousand dollars.

"Darling, what have you done?"

"I didn't do anything. As if I'd do anything in the garden without talking to you."

"That's your signature."

"I know. I'm as confused as you. It must be a forgery."

"Hey, what is this? Are you trying to pull a swifty or something? I've got a contract." The man scowled.

"Watch what you say, young fella."

The man beckoned Harry a few meters away from the other two men and Mary. "Look, I can prove I'm on the up and up. I didn't want to say anything in front of my guys, but when your wife gave me the two-thousand-dollar deposit, it nearly froze my leg off. I know for a fact that you hide your cash in the freezer, right?"

Harry was nonplussed. *What is this guy talking about? We don't have any cash in the freezer and never have.* "Look, there's been a mistake. I don't know whose. I don't want a new driveway. I liked everything the way it was. Can I have the contract and I'll contact you when I get it sorted out?"

"That's the original. I left your wife copies in triplicate. What is this? You want me to leave the only proof I have. Forget it."

Harry sighed. "Leave me your phone number then."

After the men had left, Mary asked, "What did you sort out?"

"I told him that someone was playing a nasty prank on us," Harry lied.

"Who'd do something like that? It's more than a prank. It's malicious."

"Don't worry I'll get to the bottom of it. It won't take much to put the driveway back to the way it was."

"But you lost your roses."

"I'll grow more. Don't fuss, my darling. Everything will be all right."

When Mary drifted off to sleep later that night, Harry tiptoed down to the kitchen, opened the freezer and felt around at the back until he found the thick wad of one-hundred-dollar notes. He separated them and counted exactly eight thousand dollars.

God, what was Mary doing? Where did the cash come from? Was she losing it, or worse, has she already lost it? Poor thing.

Chapter 21

ASPINE SPENT AGES LOOKING for Fiona Jeczik's weaknesses. He knew she was smart, street savvy and a vindictive bitch. Unfortunately, her father died while Aspine had been in jail, and to his knowledge, she had no living relatives, so he couldn't hurt her via that avenue. He also knew from his own experience that, despite her success, she clung to her working-class roots, and was always far more severe when interviewing conservative politicians than she was with their socialist counterparts. This, and something he recollected from a luncheon with establishment stockbrokers, Blayloch & Fitch, about the New South Wales Minister for Education, William Elmhurst, sowed the seeds of his plan: The senior partner of Blayloch and Fitch had had a little too much to drink when he said that William Elmhurst had gifted an incredibly rich coal mine to charity in 1996. Elmhurst had gone to extraordinary lengths to hide the gift. The Elmhurst family were philanthropic but also paranoid about privacy. They didn't seek any publicity or credit for their generous donations; they actually shunned it. Aspine had tucked it away in his memory bank. *People with secrets, even philanthropic secrets, are always vulnerable.*

In the years that Craig Chisholm had been Fiona's producer, he had received countless anonymous calls about corrupt politicians and businessmen that rarely resulted in a televised exposé. However, in rare instances, some resulted in stories that had rated off the radar.

The voice on the other end of the phone was a hoarse whisper. "The Crime Commission is investigating William Elmhurst, and I have the story. Are you interested?"

The Right Honorable William Elmhurst had been the member for Swanton for over thirty years and was squeaky clean. "I could be," Craig replied, without any enthusiasm. "Tell me more."

"It's top secret. The heavies in the Crime Commission are so fearful of leaks they've leased separate offices in a Melbourne building. They're investigating a Sydney politician out of Melbourne! Doesn't that tell you something? There's no signage on the doors to the offices, and there's a special team holed up there. It's real KGB stuff."

Craig fought back the urge to laugh. "Really? What's their interest in Elmhurst?"

"The government issued mining licenses to companies his son had an interest in at the time, or which he later became entitled to."

"Rubbish! It would've been obvious. The opposition would've been all over it. Besides William Elmhurst is Minister for Education and those licenses are under the Minister for Mining's watch."

"What if it wasn't so obvious? Outside of the premier, William Elmhurst is the senior sitting member in the house. He is powerful, influential and has a lot of favors owed to him."

"What are you getting at?"

"You can do a lot with companies and trusts and sometimes you have to dig through a maze before you find the real beneficiaries."

"And that's what you say the Crime Commission is doing?"

"It's not what I say. It's what I know. I have documents that prove what I'm saying."

"How did they come to be in your possession?"

"That's not important. Let's just say they fell off the back of a truck. Here's the deal. I want fifty thousand in cash, and I'll lay out the whole story for you. But if you're interested, you'll have to move quickly. I've already offered it to Channel 6, and as soon as I put the phone down, I'll be pitching it to Channel 11."

"It might be too rich for us. What else can you give me to authenticate your story? My bosses are going to need more before they approve that type of money."

The line went silent. "Are you still there?" Craig asked.

"I was thinking. Tenth floor, T & G Building. Check it out. I'll call you same time tomorrow."

Craig put the phone down and pondered what he'd just been told about William Elmhurst. It was highly improbable but not impossible. The Crime Commission was Australia's very own Star

Chamber. Witnesses who refused to answer questions could be and were imprisoned, and a witness's right to refuse to answer a question that might self-incriminate did not apply to the Crime Commission. It was a body steeped in secrecy. Coercion and fear were its two main weapons.

There was a sharp knock on the front door. When Harry Denton opened it, he was greeted by a courier holding a large plastic envelope. "Package for Mary Denton, sign here."

"Who was that?" Mary asked.

"Just a courier. He dropped off an envelope for you. What have you been buying?"

"Nothing that I can think of," Mary said, as she cut the envelope open and removed a thick book. "Oh, Harry, how could you? How could you?"

Tears were streaming down Mary's face, and Harry put his arm around her to comfort her, but she forcefully pushed him away. "Ho-how could you be so callous?"

Harry looked down at the book on the table. *Managing Alzheimer's and Dementia Behaviors.* "I don't understand."

"Are you saying that you didn't send me this dreadful book?"

"I most certainly am. I've never seen or heard of it before. Why would you think that I bought it?"

"You think I'm going around the twist. Don't think I haven't noticed how you've been looking at, and humoring me. You think I lost my car and gave the okay to dig up our driveway. I didn't! Someone is playing cruel tricks. Do you believe me?"

Harry paused for just a split second and before he could respond Mary said, "You need to think about it? Harry, don't do this to me. Please."

"I'll get to the bottom of this," Harry said, picking up the invoice. He put his cell phone on speaker mode and punched the bookshop's number in.

The woman at the bookshop was courteous but refused to help. "I'm sorry, sir, privacy laws preclude us from giving out that information to anyone other than the person who ordered the book."

"Listen, I'm Mary Denton, and the book was sent to me. Surely you can tell me who ordered it."

"Mrs. Denton? Well yes, but I'm confused. According to the paperwork, you ordered it last Wednesday. You called."

"No, I didn't," Mary snapped. "How was it paid for?"

"Visa card in your name. Do you have a Visa card?"

"Ye–yes. Tell me the details," Mary said, opening her handbag and removing the card.

"No, I can't. This is too strange. I can't give out that information."

"Let me give you my credit card number then," Mary said, reading it out.

"They're the card details I have," the woman said. "Perhaps you forgot you ordered the book."

"I did not. I did not order that horrible book. I did not. Someone must have got my credit card details off an old invoice or something."

"We always ask for the three-digit security code. That could have only come from the card. I'm sorry, are you sure you didn't forget?"

"Didn't you hear me?" Mary yelled, "I never ordered that book."

"All right, all right," the woman said. "You can send it back, and we'll credit your card. Don't upset yourself, Mrs. Denton."

Mary slammed the phone down for the first time in her life. She was gentle, loving and caring and outbursts of anger were totally out of character. She looked at Harry, and his face was clouded, but he couldn't completely hide his sympathy. "You think I ordered it; I know you do," she said, storming out of the kitchen in tears.

Chapter 22

SIR EDWIN PHILBY didn't normally answer his cell phone when he didn't recognize the caller's number. However, five calls from the same number were simply too many to ignore. "Yes," he answered, without identifying himself.

"Sir Edwin?" A female with a sophisticated voice asked.

"Who is this?"

"My name is Vanessa Edgerton. I'm one of the premier's personal assistants."

"How can I help you, Ms. Edgerton?"

"Vanessa, Sir Edwin. The premier is announcing a significant building extension to the Happy Koala Kindergarten in Toorak on Monday at two o'clock and wondered if you could attend. He apologizes for the short notice."

"It's a somewhat strange request. I'm long past the age of having my own little children. Why does the premier want me to attend?"

"You're a prominent citizen in the area, Sir Edwin, and the premier thought you should be in the official party. There'll be at least two other eminent citizens on stage with you."

"On stage?"

"Oh, I'm sorry, you thought the premier was just inviting you to attend with the parents of children. That's not the case at all. He wants you next to him, supporting him so as to speak. However, he realizes you're a busy man and will understand if you can't attend."

"Vanessa, I'm sure I can reorganize my day, and you may inform the premier that I'm pleased to accept his kind invitation. Will you confirm by email?"

There was a slight pause. "I'm actually on annual leave, Sir Edwin. The premier called me this morning and asked me to contact you. I'm sorry to say this, but he thought his minders might not approve, and he didn't want the hassle of justifying himself to them."

"I understand, don't fuss about the email. I'll be there. Will I wait for the premier's entourage or will I meet him inside?"

"The premier would like you to wait until he arrives to join the official party."

"Yes, that's fine. Please pass on my warmest regards to the premier."

"I will, Sir Edwin. You have my number, so if anything comes up, please call me."

Philby put the phone down and smiled. It was the first establishment invitation he'd received for nearly ten years and from no lesser a figure than the premier. Perhaps those who counted in the state were finally bringing him in from the cold. Had he called the premier's office he would have found that Vanessa Edgerton was one of his PAs and that she was on annual leave, but she was not the woman whom he had just spoken to.

Craig Chisholm and one of his researchers entered the T & G Building and went straight to the bank of six elevators, but when they hit level 10, there was no response. "What do you make of that, boss?"

"Don't know, Donny. I sure wasn't expecting it. It's nearly one o'clock. Let's hang around and wait for the luncheon crowd to get back. Then we'll follow them into the elevators and see what happens."

Five minutes later the foyer was crowded, and Craig and Donny squeezed into an elevator just in time to see a large, heavyset man swipe a card and level 10 light up. Two men alighted on level 10 with Craig and Donny close behind them. The heavyset man turned abruptly and said, "What do you think you're doing?"

"What do you mean?"

"You need security clearances to get onto this floor, and I know you two don't have them. What are you doing?"

"I'm sorry," Craig said. "We have an appointment with CNC Insurance. We must have got the wrong floor."

"Yeah, you sure did," the man growled, swiping his card in a slot next to the stainless-steel elevator call panel.

As the elevator doors opened the man said, "This floor's off limits to the public. Don't make the mistake of coming back because you mightn't find me so polite next time."

"I said we were sorry," Craig said. "Jeez, what are you guarding? Gold ingots or something?"

"That's none of your business, and it can be unhealthy to be too nosy," The man snarled, shunting them into the elevator. "Make sure I don't see you on this floor again."

On the way down to the ground floor, Craig said, "What did you make of that?"

"Strange. There was no signage on the double glass doors, and there were no receptionists, but security cards had to be swiped to gain entry to the offices."

"Yeah, and I noticed a number of guys with their shirtsleeves rolled up, running around with notepads and laptops. It looked to be a hive of activity."

"I noticed that, too. Don't you think it was funny that there were no women, Craig?"

"I did until that bloody G-man shoved us into the elevator. His suit coat came partially open, and I caught a glance of a shoulder holster. I have a feeling it's a boys only operation."

"Why would you need guns to investigate a politician, if, in fact, that's what they're doing?"

"I don't know, Donny. When we get back, I want you to call the building's leasing agent and see what you can find out about level 10's tenants."

Mary Denton hadn't driven her car since the day it mysteriously disappeared. The High Street Road, Armadale, strip-shopping center was only a short walk from home. It was a fine day, and she was glad to get a little time to herself as Harry had been watching her like a hawk. She literally smelled the roses as she pushed her shopping trolley down the still partially dug up driveway and onto the street. Five minutes later she was buying magazines at the newsagent's and passing the time of day with the owner. Mary didn't notice the young girl with her head buried in fitness and health magazines. Mary knew the owners and shop assistants in most of the stores, and she went into gift stores, haberdasheries and fashion boutiques relishing the opportunity to talk to people who didn't think she'd lost her marbles. After enjoying a coffee and a vanilla slice, she entered the cashmere shop. It was a tiny store but well stocked, and Mary loved the feel of cashmere. She picked up a turquoise top for the third time — it was exquisite but nearly eight hundred dollars, and she knew Harry would consider it a waste of money. Normally this wouldn't have phased her as she knew he liked to exaggerate but deep down he wouldn't object. It was just that now was not the time. The sounds of horns beeping and angry voices made her glance out the window where two male drivers were abusing each other over a parking space. She said goodbye to the owner and left the store to continue her window shopping spree. She had been gone less than a minute when the young girl who'd been in the newsagent asked, "Oh, did that lady buy that beautiful turquoise top?"

The shop assistant had seen Mary looking at the top, but she most definitely hadn't bought it. "No," she said, running out the door.

Luckily, Mary was only seventy meters along the street looking in the window of a bedding store. "What did you do with that turquoise top?" The shop owner shouted.

"Wh-what do you mean?" Mary said, taken aback.

"You know what I'm talking about. You stole it. I saw you holding it up and when you left it was gone."

"I did not."

A small crowd stopped to watch and listen to the women screaming at each other, as did two detectives who'd been tipped off about a major shoplifting gang operating in the area. At the rear of the crowd were a reporter and photographer who'd been informed of the police operation.

"Let me look in your shopping trolley!"

"I will not," Mary said, indignant that she was being accused.

"Then I'll look myself," the shop owner said, moving to pull the vinyl cover off.

"Hold on," one of the detectives said, flashing his badge. "Lady, if you know the top's not in your trolley then let me see, and then we can all get on with our lives."

"I'm not showing her," Mary said, pointing defiantly at the shop owner.

"That's fine. Just show me, now please unbutton the cover."

Mary reached down, unbuttoned the cover, and gasped in horror. There was the cashmere top, which the detective took out of the trolley and held up.

"I knew it. I knew it. Shoplifter! You tried to steal from me."

A camera flashed repeatedly, and a murmur went through the crowd.

"I-I didn't," Mary screamed. "Someone must have planted it. I would never steal anything."

"You two better come down to the station," the detective said.

"I can't," the shop owner said. "I have to get back and look after my store. I'll come down and make a statement after I close up. Can I have my top back please?"

"No, you'll have to wait; it's evidence."

Mary could neither think nor talk. The other detective took her gently by the elbow. "Come on," he said.

No one noticed the man standing across the road. Why would they? There was nothing special, noticeable or different about him — other than the leather gloves he was wearing on a warm spring day.

Chapter 23

DOUGLAS ASPINE HAD A special hate for Jasmine Bartlett, the woman who had stolen more than eight years of his life. Her eldest son, Jack, was now eighteen and Sam, her other son, was fifteen. With the help of Mick McHugh, Aspine knew more about Jack's daily schedule than Jack himself. Jack was the means by which Aspine would ensure that Jasmine Bartlett suffered unimaginable pain, and if for any reason this failed, he would have Sam as a fallback.

Jack Bartlett was an average looking young man who had inherited his late father's looks rather than his mother's incredible beauty. He had been a brilliant secondary school student who had his pick of under-graduate courses and had surprisingly chosen civil engineering in preference to the more popular law and medicine. It was late afternoon when Jack finished his last lecture for the day at Melbourne University. He walked briskly to the Eastern Precinct Car Park in Carlton worried that he'd be late for his shift at McDonald's in the outer eastern suburb of Scoresby. As Jack approached his car he saw a stunning young girl, tears streaming from her hauntingly beautiful aquamarine eyes.

"What's wrong?" He asked.

She pointed to the flat rear tire on the little red Toyota parked next to his gleaming blue Ford. "I don't know how to change it, and I have to get home to my sick grandmother." She whimpered. "I promised I'd fill her prescriptions and cook dinner tonight. She's very ill."

"Have you called the RACV?"

"I'm a student. I can't afford the RACV."

Jack glanced down at his watch and sighed. "I'll change it for you. It'll only take a few minutes."

"Oh, you're sweet," the young girl gushed. "Thank you so much. I'm Anneka Nordstrom."

She had light brown hair with blonde streaks, pronounced cheekbones and full lips. She was wearing a tight lemon t-shirt and faded blue jeans that accentuated her tiny waist, but it was her eyes that drew and held Jack.

"I'm Ja-Jack, Jack Bartlett," he said. "I'm running late too. Can you pop your boot?"

As Jack changed the tire, Anneka chatted incessantly asking questions about what he was studying and what his personal interests were while continuing to thank him profusely. "Here's your problem," Jack said, removing the wheel and pointing to a nail in the tire. She bent down and leaned forward to look at it. Jack glimpsed a lacy lemon bra and just enough flesh to hold his eyes as if they were in a vice. "You-you need to ge-get the spare fixed as soon as you can."

"I'll do it tomorrow. You have a great looking car," she said.

"Thanks. It's old, but I've spent a lot of time restoring it."

Ten minutes later Jack was finished and rubbing his dirty hands together to get rid of the grit from the tire. "You'll be fine now." he smiled. "I hope you make it home in time."

"Thank you, thank you, thank you," Anneka said, stepping forward and placing her hands on his shoulders while kissing him on the cheek. It was more than just a peck, and her firm breasts brushed his chest.

"Glad I could help." Jack grinned sheepishly.

"I'm going to buy you lunch or a drink." Anneka smiled, scribbling on a piece of paper. "Here's my number. Call me."

"You don't have to do that."

"I know I don't have to. I want to. I'll understand if you're too busy studying though."

"I'll call," Jack responded in a flash, and they both burst out laughing.

As Anneka drove out of the car park, she rolled down her window. "Thanks again, Jack. I'm looking forward to your call."

Jack sat behind the wheel of his car, stunned. He felt like he'd been hit by a tornado and his hormones were running wild. The girl had been alluring, almost teasing and yet innocent, but it was her eyes that fascinated him — it was not only their unique color but that they never seemed to blink — that was what had made it so hard to hold her gaze.

When Donny called the leasing agent of the T & G Building to enquire about the level 10 tenants he was told: "I'm sorry, sir, we've been sworn to secrecy."

"I'm just trying to get the cleaning contract. Can you just give me a name and phone number?"

"Sorry, I'm not authorized to do that."

"Jeez, well what business are they in?"

"I'm sorry."

The agent put the phone down and smiled. Mick McHugh had told him he would get a call seeking information about the tenant, and when he did, the precise way in which he was to respond. McHugh was not someone to be crossed, and the agent had complied to the letter with his instructions.

Sir Edwin Philby had always been a stickler for punctuality, so it was no surprise when he arrived fifteen minutes early at the Happy Koala Kindergarten. He sat out the front in his car reading the newspaper almost oblivious to the sound of little children playing only a few meters away. At 1:55 he was becoming concerned because there were no parents milling around at the entrance to the kindergarten, and there was no sign of the premier and his entourage. Perhaps the function had been canceled, and Vanessa Edgerton had forgotten to advise him.

How rude and annoying.

He punched her number into his cell phone, but strangely there was no ring tone or voicemail. He waited another five minutes before getting out of his car and striding purposefully toward the entrance gate. Surely the premier's office would have notified the kindergarten staff if there had been a change of time or a cancellation.

Chapter 24

THE HAND ON HIS shoulder was heavy. Sir Edwin swung around to see two burly men dressed in ill-fitting suits and wearing hats. Immediately behind them were television crews, reporters, and photographers. "Inspector Ron Ireland, sexual crimes squad," the larger of the two men said, showing his badge. "You're under arrest, Sir Edwin. You have the right to–"

"You bloody fool, what are you talking about?"

"We have reason to believe that you have been watching and trafficking in child porn and–"

"I'm Sir Edwin Philby. I'm a pillar of the community, you idiot. I wouldn't dream of doing something like that. I'll have your job. Where did you get such a stupid idea?"

"We've tracked emails with pics attached to and from your email address. They were enough to obtain search warrants and my men are searching your premises and offices."

"You're doing what? I haven't seen any warrants."

"Your cook and secretary have. Now come on."

"What were you doing in front of the kindergarten?" one of the reporters shouted.

"Yeah, why would you sit in front of a kindergarten?" another yelled.

"You don't know what you're talking about," Sir Edwin snarled. "I'm here at the invite of the premier."

"That's enough," Inspector Ireland said to the reporters.

"You're making a big mistake," Sir Edwin said, as the police shoved him in the back of a waiting divvy van manned by two uniformed policemen. "I have important contacts in this city. Before this is over, you're going to rue this day."

That night Aspine channel surfed watching the news. Every channel covered Sir Edwin's arrest and the exchange he'd had with the reporters. He looked shocked, angry and under severe stress. The following morning the arrest was on the front page of both Melbourne's dailies. The police had said very little, but there were rumors on the internet that thousands of kiddie porn pics had been found on Sir Edwin's computers, and shocking photographs had been hidden around his house. Aspine hadn't had sex since his escape and nor did he have any desire. Watching the news and reading what the dailies were saying about Sir Edwin was far more satisfying than any sexual encounter could ever be. Sir Edwin was finished; he would end up in jail shunned by the community as there was nothing lower than a trafficker and purveyor of kiddie porn. Aspine realized, that with time, computer experts might eventually prove the pics were planted on Sir Edwin's computer, but he would never regain his standing in the community, and would forever be thought of as a pedophile.

The call to Craig Chisholm was right on time. "Do you believe me now?" the rasping voice asked.

"I didn't find anything other than there are some people occupying the floor of a city building who are paranoid about secrecy. I guess there are plenty of floors like that in this city."

"Bullshit! With no signage in the foyer or on the door. With elevators that bypass level 10 without a security swipe card? I get the impression you're not interested, and if that's the case just let me know because your competitors sure are."

"I'm interested. I just need more."

"All right, but this is the last information you get without producing some cash. Get your lawyers to look at the share register of Clean Coal Limited and then search one of its larger shareholders, Benefish Proprietary Limited. Don't take too long though, cause the guys at Channel 6 are hot for this story, and if they weren't penny-pinching, I'd already have sold it to them. Oh, and just in case you try the same stunt, it's fifty grand in cash, and I won't take a cent less. *Capiche?*"

"Yeah, yeah."

"I'll call the same time tomorrow."

Harry Denton pleaded with the police not to charge Mary, but they were paranoid about the Office of Police Integrity and the Victoria's newly created Independent Broad Based Anti-Corruption Commission. The days when police officers could use their discretion to either warn or charge someone were long gone and Big Brother was always looking over their shoulders. From reading and watching the news, it was easy to gain the impression that there were more police in Victoria investigating other police, than police investigating criminals. The local *Leader* newspaper ran the story with a photo of Mary and the shop owner arguing heatedly in High Street Road. Mary had sworn to Harry that she hadn't taken the cashmere top and someone must have planted it. She was devastated, and the article in the *Leader* had been like a dagger through her heart. They never missed a Sunday morning service at their local Presbyterian Church, but Mary refused to go out anymore, too embarrassed to face her friends and fellow parishioners. She confined herself to the house forsaking the charitable and community work she'd undertaken for decades.

Harry was distraught. He loved Mary so much, and he blamed himself for not seeing the encroaching dementia that she was clearly suffering. He recalled her losing and misplacing keys, forgetting appointments and going out without locking the house. He'd paid scant attention to these occasional lapses because he'd also become forgetful, and had just put it down as part of the aging process. Close friends had suggested that Mary might need the care a nursing home could provide. Harry could not imagine waking up without Mary next to him, but perhaps she would be better off in a nursing home.

I hate the thought, but am I being selfish? Wouldn't she be better off with professionals looking after her? For the first time, he worried about predeceasing her. *What will my poor darling do if we're still in this house and I die? It might be better to get her into a nursing home now.*

Chapter 25

RETIRED DETECTIVE BILL MULLER was amazed. He had interviewed Sir Edwin Philby about the hit and run attempt on Douglas Aspine's life and later about Kerry Bartlett's suicide. Philby had been pompous and full of himself, but after all, he was a knight of the realm, and that carried a lot of status. Muller prided himself on his judgment, honed by nearly forty years of policing, and was certain he knew the signs of pedophilia having grilled many pedophiles. Philby had not exhibited any of those signs, and Muller knew that he was either incredibly cunning or had been set up, as he was bleating to anyone who would listen. Muller was so intrigued that he made a few phone calls to mates still on the force and learned that the evidence was damning; thousands of disgusting photographs had been found on Philby's computers, and he'd been arrested skulking around a kindergarten. His claim that the premier had invited him to a function at the kindergarten was an outright lie. There was no function, and the PA he claimed to have spoken to, Vanessa Edgerton, denied ever speaking to him. He hadn't used his normal email address when trafficking pics but had created a Gmail account in the name of kiddieluva. According to Muller's contacts, "Sir Edwin Philby was one helluva sick son of a bitch."

It had taken Jack Bartlett forty-eight hours to build up the courage to call Anneka. He need not have worried. She teased him about how long he had taken. They agreed to meet up for brunch on Saturday morning at Albert Park. Jack was already waiting in the restaurant when Anneka arrived wearing a summery white dress, with a green and gold flowery pattern and matching white half wedge sandals that showed off her long, toned legs. As he rose to greet her, she kissed him lightly on the lips, and he felt his face burning.

"Hello. Did you have enough time to get your grandmother's medicine?" he asked.

"Thanks to you I did," Anneka said, putting her hand on top of his. "I told her how wonderful you were."

Jack's heart beat a little faster. "It was nothing. I never asked you. What are you studying?"

"Business Studies but not at Melbourne. I'm at Monash but was trying to get a transfer the day we met in the car park."

"Monash is an excellent university. Why do you want to transfer?"

"Yes." She laughed. "It is, but Melbourne is so much more prestigious. Internationally it is recognized as our finest learning institution."

A waitress appeared. Anneka ordered a green smoothie, and Jack copied her, even though he would've preferred bacon and eggs. "Were you born here?" he asked.

"No, in Sweden but I've been here since I was six."

"How old are you?"

"Eighteen," She lied. "And you?"

"The same. Where do you live?"

"Mt Eliza. It's beautiful, but it's so far from everything. I love the beaches and greenery though. Life is full of trade-offs, isn't it?"

The waitress brought their smoothies, and Jack was pleasantly surprised by the taste. "This is quite sweet," he said. "There must be a lot of fruit in it to counter the taste of the vegetables."

"Sweet, just like you." Anneka smiled.

As they left the restaurant, she reached down and took Jack's hand. "Do you have time for a walk along the beach?"

"I have all day." He laughed.

"Hmmm, so do I."

Craig Chisholm's investigations into Benefish Proprietary Limited did just enough to pique his curiosity. In early 2003 the New South Wales government had issued Clean Coal Limited with an exploration license for coal over privately owned barren land in the west of the state and subsequently a grant for development approval. Title to the property had been in the name of William Elmhurst for many years, but in 1995 it was transferred to Benefish Pty Ltd, a company that appeared to have no connection with the Elmhurst Family. The development grant added significantly to the value of the property, and in late 2003, ownership was transferred to Clean Coal Limited for a consideration of sixty million dollars satisfied by issuing six percent of the shares in Clean Coal Limited to Benefish Proprietary Limited. Fifty of the hundred shares in Benefish Proprietary Limited were owned by an accountant's nominee company and the other fifty by a lawyer's nominee company. Clean Coal Limited had been incredibly successful and paid ever increasing dividends from 2000 and Benefish Pty Limited's six percent was now worth close to two hundred million. Whether William Elmhurst was involved in anything untoward or criminal, could only be determined by finding out who the accountant's and lawyer's nominee companies were holding the shares in Benefish Proprietary Limited for.

Chapter 26

THE MELBOURNE MAGISTRATES COURT was a hive of activity, and it was nothing for a sitting magistrate to hear more than a hundred cases in a day. Defendants charged with causing a public nuisance, offensive behavior, assault, shoplifting, burglary, driving offenses and a plethora of other criminal charges predominantly were unrepresented and pleaded guilty. By necessity, justice was incredibly swift. However, a small percentage of defendants always pleaded not guilty, some of whom were represented by attorneys skilled in the workings of the magistrates' courts. Sometimes the magistrates were even swifter and more brutal with those defendants, deeming they were wasting the court's time.

Mary Denton was represented by senior and junior counsel together with their instructing lawyer, a level of representation almost unheard of in the lower courts. Senior counsel had examined the evidence and advised Mary to plead guilty, after which, and because of her long and flawless record, he would implore the court not to record a conviction, but she would not hear of it. Because of her embarrassment, she had also fought against calling character witnesses, but Harry had insisted, and there were more than twenty witnesses on the witness list prepared to speak glowingly about Mary. The prosecutor read out the charge and then called the shop owner and the two detectives as witnesses.

Senior counsel cross-examined the shop owner asking her if she had actually seen Mary put the cashmere top in her shopping trolley, and whether it was possible that someone had planted it. "No and yes. It's possible but unlikely," she responded.

The magistrate was impatiently drumming his fingers on the bench. Not guilty pleas like this made it impossible for him to complete his list — impossible if he didn't bring them to an end that was. Senior counsel called the first of Mary's character witnesses and was about to call the second when the magistrate rapped his gavel on the bench. "Guilty, but with no conviction recorded and the defendant will put two hundred dollars in the poor box."

Mary started to stand up and protest, but her lawyer took her arm and gently pulled her back down. "I really must protest, Your Honor," senior counsel said, though he was quite pleased.

"Protest all you like, counsel." The magistrate chuckled. "You can always appeal if you don't like my ruling."

"I want to appeal," Mary whimpered, but her legal team was not listening, and for them, the matter was closed.

A *Herald-Sun* reporter sat at the back of the court furiously typing on his notepad. With luck, his article about there being one law for the rich and another for the poor would appear on page three of tomorrow's paper.

In the week that had elapsed since Jack Bartlett had brunch with Anneka Nordstrom, they had been inseparable. Jack had taken girls out before but had never had a girlfriend, and now he was totally infatuated. They had gone to the movies and bumped into some students in Jack's class who wouldn't normally give him the time of day, but had fallen over themselves to get introduced to Anneka. He couldn't have cared less about them, but his chest swelled with pride when he was with her. He would've had to have been blind not to notice the admiring and sometimes lecherous glances that she attracted. She was not only aesthetically and physically perfect, but had a great personality and was happy going to places that he could afford on his limited budget. It was early evening when they came out of Subway holding hands and giggling as they strolled over to Jack's car.

"I'm sorry," she said. "You'll have to drop me back at my car. I promised granny that I'd be home while it was still daylight so I could take her for a walk. She's in a wheelchair and hardly gets out at all."

"I understand," Jack said, putting his arms around her waist and drawing her to him. They kissed passionately, and Jack held her tighter, thrusting with his lower body. His hormones were totally out of control, and he was breathing heavily.

"Whoa, slow down, tiger." Anneka laughed, gently pushing him away.

He looked mortified. "I–I'm sorry."

"You don't have to be sorry. I want you just as much but this is not the time or place. When it happens, I want to remember it for the rest of my life. It will be the first time for me," She lied.

"Me too."

"I'm glad," she said. "I'd hate it if you were one of those playboys."

"Me? A playboy? You're kidding."

"Why not? You're a good-looking young man, but you're mine. If I catch you looking at another woman, I'll castrate you." She giggled.

On the short drive to her car, Anneka held Jack's hand and said, "Do you want to arrange something for next weekend?"

"Do you mean–"

"I do." She giggled. "But only if you want to as well."

Jack's out of control hormones had completely taken over his addled brain, and he gasped, "I want to. I want to."

Fiona Jeczik listened intently as Craig Chisholm told her about anonymous calls and The Crime Commission's investigation of William Elmhurst. "I knew it," she said. "Squeaky clean Bill Elmhurst is too good to be true."

"We don't know that yet," Craig protested. "Don't let your dislike for the conservatives cloud your judgment."

"It never has. There's far too much smoke here for there not to be some fire. I can feel it in my veins."

"Fifty thousand's an awful lot of money."

"I'll take care of it," Fiona said. "Set something up with this guy and let's see what he's got. In the meantime, I want you to call those accountants and lawyers fronting Benefish Proprietary Limited and find out if they act for Elmhurst personally. Tell the receptionists that you're an insurance broker and Elmhurst asked you to call about a building you're insuring. If you're put through to a partner just hang up, that'll almost be enough confirmation for me that he pushed a license and development grant through the parliament to feather his own nest."

Craig sighed. "That's nowhere near enough. It could be a coincidence. It could be that Elmhurst made a sale of the land to someone with the same accountants and lawyers."

"Did you see the three pigs' just fly past my window?" Fiona sneered. "Craig, you've been with me for nearly fifteen years. How many times has this nose ever been wrong?"

"Never."

"Exactamundo, and it's not wrong now. Get all you can from this snitch and start setting up an interview with Elmhurst. Tell his minders that it's to celebrate his thirty years in Parliament. He's not going to know what hit him."

"As you wish," Craig said. "I have a bad feeling about this."

"You've had bad feelings before and been wrong." Fiona laughed. "Face it, you're just a worry wart. I love you for looking after my back, but my gut instinct's never let me down, and it's not about to now."

Chapter 27

DOUGLAS ASPINE HAD PLENTY of time on his hands and was working out regularly in the gym. With the exercise and improved diet, he was slowly gaining weight and could now look at himself in the mirror without feeling ill. Sonchai had done a superb job removing the excess stomach skin, and the scar was barely noticeable. Mick McHugh was particularly adept at implementing his plans, and Aspine knew that two of his enemies were suffering badly. Sir Edwin Philby was a figure of ridicule and disgust, and would most likely lose his knighthood.

Better still, he knew the self-righteous Harry Denton would be going through his own private hell. The *Herald Sun* had published a page three story with a picture of Mary Denton highlighting the lenient treatment she'd received from the court. The reporter was appalled and suggested the Director of Public Prosecutions appeal the leniency of the sentence. Aspine knew Harry Denton valued honesty above all other qualities, and it was something he preached to others, but he now had a wife who was a known thief.

What is old Harry thinking? Is he thinking of having his wife committed? Is he watching her like a hawk? Does he humor her and does she respond in anger? How is their relationship holding up? Do they still talk to each other?

Bill Muller read the same article and wondered what was going on. He had gotten to know Harry and Mary Denton as a result of his Mercury Properties related investigations and knew them to be an honest, loving and caring couple.

"Does old age make you a thief?" he pondered aloud. *If it happened to Mary could it also happen to me when I reach her age?*

No, it was too ridiculous to even contemplate. Harry might be careful with his pennies, but he'd had an extremely successful business career and invested wisely. Mary had the means to buy anything she wanted, so where was the logic in her stealing clothes with a measly value of eight hundred dollars? It just didn't ring true.

Muller went out to the kitchen and made himself a strong black coffee before sitting down in what he called his *thinking chair* and pondering the recent strange events. It was a large, old fabric lounge chair and while it had seen better days, Muller found it very comfortable. Other than Fiona Jeczik, who was a national television star, he had not seen or heard of any of the players in the Mercury Properties debacle for nearly ten years. Now, in the space of just a few months, Douglas Aspine had staged a daring escape from Changi, Sir Edwin Philby had been charged with trafficking kiddie porn, and Mary Denton had been found guilty of shoplifting. Was it just coincidence or was Douglas Aspine pulling strings from an overseas hideaway? Bill Muller had often been perplexed when he was a detective, and it was usually when he was close to a solution but didn't know it. The same feeling was nagging away at him now, but there was no solution in sight.

The instructions to Craig Chisholm were explicit. He was to go to the Flagstaff Gardens on Tuesday at midnight and was to enter from the Latrobe Street entrance. He was to come alone with no cameras or recording devices, but he could bring a flashlight and would be allowed ten minutes to peruse the documents and determine their authenticity. Craig had objected saying he wasn't going to carry fifty thousand in cash around the streets of Melbourne at that time of night without security. After a short exchange, the raspy-voiced man had agreed to let Craig bring one of his assistants and a security guard. Late night clandestine meetings with informants were nothing new for Craig, but they were usually held in seedy ill-lit bars or restaurants.

Jack could hardly eat and picked nervously at his steak, but Anneka didn't seem to be having any problems with her crispy flathead fillets. "These are to die for," she said. "This is a nice restaurant, Jack."

"It-it's a special night."

"You're romantic." Anneka smiled, placing her hand over his. "Is there something wrong with your steak?"

"No, I'm just not as hungry as I thought I was."

"There's no pressure, my darling. If it happens, it happens, please don't stress."

Jack had never organized a tryst before, and the butterflies in his stomach were creating their own mayhem. *No pressure? I nearly died of embarrassment buying condoms at the supermarket while that pimply faced, checkout girl smirked at me. And I felt uncomfortable booking the room in the names of Mr. & Mrs. Bartlett. I'm dreading having to show my license when checking into the motel knowing the receptionist will look at my address and know I'm not a traveler.*

"I'm fine. I just don't have much of an appetite."

Jack hardly spoke on the short drive to the motel in the upmarket beachside suburb of Brighton, but Anneka babbled away seemingly oblivious to his discomfit. It was a four-star motel, and two hundred dollars was a large part of Jack's weekly budget. The receptionist swiped his credit card and took a photocopy of his license while explaining that there was milk in the fridge for tea and coffee, and a fully stocked minibar. Fortunately, she paid them scant attention only adding that checkout was 10 A.M.

As Jack pushed the motel room door open, he let out an almighty sigh of relief.

"Are you all right, darling?"

"I'm fine," He lied, reaching out and drawing her to him. He kissed her hard, but she gently pushed him away.

"We have all night." she smiled. "Why don't you jump into bed while I go to the bathroom and get changed into something a little more comfortable?"

Jack threw off his clothes except for his jocks and put the packet of condoms on the table next to the bed. Five minutes later Anneka came out of the bathroom. She was wearing a black negligee, a G-string and a pair of stilettoes and nothing else. "My god," he gasped. "You're beautiful."

"You like?" She demurely asked, as if it was possible to be demure in the way she was dressed.

"Come here," he pleaded, his throat parched.

Jack rolled on top of her thrusting wildly while roughly fondling her breasts and kissing her passionately. "Slow down, big boy, we have all night."

She rolled him over on his side and ran her hands teasingly over his body. "You've still got your jocks on," she said, holding her hands up. "Take my negligee off. Be gentle and don't rip it."

It's all right for her to say slow down. If I don't do it in the next five minutes, I'm going to do it anyway — without her.

Jack reached over and grabbed a condom fumbling with the foil wrapping before finally tearing it open. He tried to put it on but it wouldn't unroll and the harder he tried, the less progress he made. He was fighting with his brain, sending it instructions to stop himself ejaculating, but knew he was fighting a losing fight.

"Here let me help," Anneka said. Taking the condom from him, she deftly rolled it down his shaft.

She didn't move as he pumped away like a wild horse and fifteen seconds later let out an almighty scream and rolled off her. "I'm sorry."

"Why?"

"I didn't last very long. It mustn't have been much fun for you."

"It was fine, big boy, and we have all night for me," Anneka said, curling up under his arm. By the time they checked out in the morning, Jack had lost count of the number of times they'd made love.

Chapter 28

MARY DENTON REFUSED TO leave the house, and she and Harry hardly spoke. She felt violated and far too ashamed to attend the many regular community groups she'd been helping over the years. Harry had been dying to ask her about the cash in the freezer, and regularly checked that it was still there, but couldn't find the right time to pop the question. The harmony and trust they'd enjoyed were lost, and Mary resented Harry's close overseeing of her every movement. She was angry with Harry and his condescending comments, and unable to leave the house for fear of bumping into someone she might know. There was nothing Harry wouldn't do for Mary. He still loved her deeply, but she wanted only two things from him — his trust and his belief in what she had told him. Instead, he treated her like she was a senile idiot, not fit to cross the street without his help. She silently seethed, knowing that someone had organized the disdainful acts she had been falsely accused of, unable to convince Harry of the authenticity of her claims or sanity.

It was a bleak night. Craig Chisholm and his two offsiders felt the full force of the wind on their faces as they toiled up Latrobe Street. The streets were deserted other than a few raucous drunks and a beggar rattling a tin signed *ex-Vietnam veteran* in their faces. The noise coming from the Flagstaff Gardens was a crescendo of howling wind and rustling trees. Huge hundred-year-old Moreton Bay Figs, elms, eucalypts, palms, cypresses and a variety of other species joined to form a dark moving canopy that enveloped the normally well-lit gardens. Perhaps the fierce winds had caused a blackout, but for some nagging reason, Craig thought the person they were meeting had had something to do with it. They trudged along one of the paths without seeing or hearing anyone in the gardens before noticing a light flicker off and on in the distance. Craig checked the layout of the gardens at the weekend and knew the light was coming from near the obelisk known as the *Pioneers' Memorial,* and he led the way in a quick jog toward it.

"You're late," the raspy and instantly recognizable voice yelled.

Craig jumped and took an instant to work out where the voice had come from. He was tall, about 190 centimeters, and dressed in a black tracksuit, black sneakers and eerily, a black ski mask.

"Jesus," Craig said. "You look like a fucking Jihadist. You frightened the shit out of me."

"You'll live, Mr. Chisholm. Now you know why I couldn't meet you in a bar or restaurant. If certain people knew what I was doing, I'd be dead. Here. Here's the envelope. You can get some protection behind that statue but make sure the wind doesn't scatter any of the papers. If it does, the fifty's still mine."

"Obelisk, not statue."

"What, what are you talking about?"

"Forget it," Craig hollered. "Are you alone?"

"Do you think I'm stupid?" the man replied, flicking his torch on and in a few seconds two other lights flicked off and on. "And, by the way, they're packing real heat, magnums, not like that fucking toy on your security guard's hip. You've got ten minutes to check the documents. Don't waste it."

The security guard did his best to hold the documents still behind the obelisk while Craig and Donny attempted to skim read them under the flashlight. There were copies of bank statements, trust deeds, company constitutions, dividend statements and tax returns. "What do you think, Donny?"

"They look authentic."

"And damning for the member. My worry is that they're just too perfect. Don't you feel that?"

"Sorry, boss. No, I don't. I think this is huge."

"You've had ten minutes," raspy voice shouted. "Are you buying or do I meet with one of your competitors' tomorrow night?"

Craig knew that the package had been hawked to Channel 11 and they were interested. He also knew Fiona would kill him if they scooped her. He looked over at the security guard. "Give him the satchel. It's all there, but you can count it if you want."

The man opened the satchel, counted how many hundred-dollar notes there were in one bundle and then the number of bundles. "I didn't think you'd cheat me, but it always pays to check," he said, flicking his torch off and on twice. "I'll be off now. Don't worry. My men will be joining me. It's been a pleasure doing business with you, Mr. Chisholm. Goodbye."

"Yeah," Craig muttered, as the man disappeared into the darkness and screaming winds.

"Funny, that he didn't pat us down for wires," Donny yelled.

"Not really," Craig replied. "He hardly said anything, and most of what he did say would've been drowned out by the noise. Let's get out of here. It's bloody spooky."

Jack Bartlett was completely besotted by Anneka and spent his days wandering around in a love and lust induced daze. He found it nigh on impossible to concentrate on his studies, knowing that at the end of the day he would see her and they would make love. They did it in the back seat of his car. They did it in secluded parklands. They did it in cheap hotels and motels — they did it everywhere. Anneka was adventurous and bought a modern-day *Kama Sutra* determined that they would try every position. She had barely moved the first time they had made love, but in the short time since, she had morphed into a cross between a contortionist and a dominatrix. Any inhibitions that had held her back on that first night disappeared in her desire to experiment sexually. She did things with her fingertips and mouth that drove Jack crazy, and then told him explicitly what she wanted him to do to her. He'd been surprised at first but then recalled reading something about the Swedes being totally uninhibited, and silently blessed the flat tire that had led to this state of perpetual bliss.

The St Kilda motel was cheap and seedy, but the sheets were clean, and Jack and Anneka didn't worry about the décor. "I have a surprise for you." She smiled.

"Not another hundred positions book." Jack laughed.

"Better," she said, holding up two little pills. "Ecstasy."

"I don't do drugs." Jack frowned. "Where'd you get them?"

"On campus, from a girlfriend. She said that she and her boyfriend use them when they're making out and it intensifies the pleasure. They're not addictive, and according to her, there are no nasty after effects. What do you think?"

"I dunno. Just don't like the idea of doing drugs. Besides, I think what we have is fantastic and can't see how it could get any better."

"Oh, that's so nice," Anneka said, looking disappointed. "You know me, I just like to experiment, but if you don't want to, I'll just flush these down the sink."

"No, no, let's do it, but just this once. I don't want us to end up a couple of desperate druggies," Jack said, half filling two glasses with water.

Anneka passed Jack a pill, clinked glasses, put her hand to her mouth and said, "I hope they're all that they're cracked up to be," but she didn't swallow anything other than the water.

Forty-five minutes later after they'd made love, Anneka said, "Do you feel any different?"

"Nope. What about you?"

"Nothing."

"I think your girlfriend must have given you sugar coated pills or something. I'm not fussed; I didn't really want to do drugs. I'm going to have a quick nap," Jack said, as Anneka nestled into his chest and ran her fingers across his torso.

Jack didn't know how long he had dozed, but when he woke up, he felt fantastic, euphoric and was rock hard. "God, I feel great. I've never felt this good. Get a feel of this," he gasped, grabbing Anneka's hand and wrapping it around his erection, something he hadn't been forward enough to do before. "What about you?"

"I'm on cloud nine," Anneka lied. "I'm so wet. Do me, do me hard, baby."

When Jack woke up the following morning everything, even the grotty motel room looked good, and he still felt on top of the world. He nudged Anneka, "Good morning, sleepy head," he said, cupping a breast in his hand.

She was relieved. She knew that sometimes Ecstasy users could suffer huge letdowns, but one look at Jack's face told her he was still on a high. "You were very amorous last night," she said, stretching her lithe body.

"Wasn't it fun? Can you get any more of those little pills?"

Chapter 29

BILL MULLER WAS SURPRISED when he answered the phone to find it was his contact on the force. "Bill, I thought you'd like to know that Sir Edwin Philby's lawyers got an order from the court and one of their forensic computer experts has been looking at his computers."

"So?"

"He found that the Gmail address that Sir Edwin denied creating was set up at a computer café."

"So, anyone could've have done it and then used the address to traffic kiddie porn pics."

"Yep, and all the pics on Sir Edwin's computers appear to have been downloaded on one day."

"It's a frame-up?"

"Could be. We've traced the calls that Sir Edwin claimed came from Vanessa Edgerton to a prepaid cell phone."

"Far out. Are you dropping the charges?"

"The Director of Public Prosecutions is looking at the evidence but the damage has already been done, and shit always sticks. No matter what happens, there'll always be whispers about him being a sleaze-bag and pedophile. If it's a setup, I'd hate to be on the wrong side of the vicious bastard who orchestrated it."

"Thanks," Muller said, knowing there was only one person he'd ever met who was smart enough and vicious enough to have set it up.

Craig Chisholm called in forensic accounting and legal experts to inspect the copies of the documents that he'd bought off raspy voice. Before Fiona interviewed William Elmhurst, Craig wanted a hundred percent guarantee that the documents were authentic. The documents confirmed that the lawyers and accountants nominee companies held the shares in Benefish Proprietary Limited on behalf of a company controlled by William Elmhurst's eldest son, Devlin, which acted as trustee of the Elmhurst Charitable Trust Fund. A copy of the trust deed showed that there were charitable beneficiaries but the primary beneficiaries were William Elmhurst's children and their issue, and that distributions were solely at the discretion of the trustee. Bank statements in the name of the Elmhurst Charitable Trust Fund showed deposits corresponding precisely with the amounts that Clean Coal Limited had paid to Benefish Proprietary Limited as dividends. Payments out of the fund corresponded with the Clean Coal dividend deposits. Copies of Devlin Elmhurst's bank statements showed that the same amounts appeared as deposits in his account.

On the face of it, it looked like William Elmhurst had attempted to hide his ownership of a tract of land rich in coal, and then used his influence to ensure that an exploration license and development permits were issued by the New South Wales Government, thus exponentially increasing the value of the land. Clean Coal Limited had then acquired the land by issuing shares to Benefish Proprietary Limited and had paid a dividend on those shares every year since that had eventually found its way into Devlin Elmhurst's bank account. It was an open and shut case of monumental corruption. Far too open and shut for Craig Chisholm's liking.

Fiona Jeczik couldn't understand Craig's reticence when everything she'd heard and seen seemed to confirm William Elmhurst's guilt. "I don't understand your concern." She sighed. "We've gone with far less in the past, and you haven't objected."

"It's too pat," Craig said. "Too perfect. Out of thin air, it's handed to us on a plate. This guy says the documents fell off the back of a truck, and when I meet him he's wearing a face mask, so we have no idea who he really is. Usually, we know the snitch, and invariably it's a whistleblower close to or working in the perp's office. Worse, we can't authenticate the documents. Doesn't it strike you as just a little strange?"

"Not really, didn't he tell you that he'd be dead if he was found out? There's been plenty of snitches killed for far less than the millions involved in this cozy scam."

"Please. You're talking about a member of parliament. When was the last time you heard about a politician running around setting up a hit?" Craig laughed.

"You don't know who else is involved. Elmhurst might be the tip of the iceberg. Anyhow, what do you mean about not verifying the authenticity of the documents? I thought the lawyers said they were kosher and the accountants traced the Clean Coal dividends final resting place to the grubby Devlin Elmhurst's bank account."

"The trust deeds are private documents, so there are no public records that can be examined to verify them. The accountants can hardly take copies of someone else's bank statements along to the bank and say, 'Could you please just check these and let me know if they're true copies of the originals?' The lawyers said the documents have been properly stamped and look authentic, but could also be skillfully prepared forgeries. The accountants said the same about the bank statements and other financial records they examined. I wanted a one hundred percent guarantee and instead got *maybes* with added disclaimers to protect their asses."

"What did you really expect, Craig? God, they're lawyers and accountants trained in the art of avoiding any and all responsibility. What's that quaint little get-out clause they use? All care and no responsibility." Fiona laughed. "Why would anyone want to give us false documents? Master forgers don't come cheap, and they're not listed in the White Pages. I did a bit of my own checking, and if those documents are forgeries, they'd have cost close to a hundred thousand. That's double what you paid the snitch, so where's the logic in that? They're authentic."

"You've made a lot of enemies exposing scams over the years. Why couldn't it be one of them setting you up?"

"Most wouldn't be smart enough and, even if they were, I can't think of one who'd outlay a hundred thousand to do it. You said this guy had two bodyguards with him. He's the genuine article all right."

"You're going ahead with the interview?"

"Sure am. Tell the Right Honorable William Elmhurst that we're doing a doco looking back at the thirty years he's served the good people of New South Wales."

"Will you at least be careful, Fiona?"

"I always am." She smiled. "That's why I've lasted so long in this business. I want you and your team to keep digging right up until the minute I start the interview. If you find anything tangible to support your concerns I'll make it a genuine program to celebrate his political life. You won't find anything though because he's a bloody crook born to a life of privilege."

Craig shook his head. "You're the most influential and powerful woman in television. You don't have to do this."

"That's exactly why I have to do it. After all these years you still don't get it. Exposing crooks like Elmhurst is why I got where I am, and if I stop, I'll be just another bloody hack. No thanks!"

Chapter 30

JASMINE BARTLETT WAS PLEASED Jack had found a girl-friend but was worried that he was neglecting his studies. He'd never stayed out all night before, but now it was a regular occurrence on Fridays and Saturdays. She was reluctant to say anything as she knew her little boy was turning into a man. The photos that Jack had shown her of Anneka were stunning, and Jasmine asked him to invite her home for dinner. Jack explained that Anneka was shy when it came to meeting people, but he was working on it. Jasmine had never seen her son as happy, and the last thing she wanted to be was a wet blanket, but she couldn't let him neglect university. "Jack, why haven't you been attending lectures lately?"

"Don't fuss, Mom." He laughed. "I'm doing them on the net."

"But you're hardly ever home."

"Trust me, it's under control," he said, kissing her on the forehead. "I'm heading off to an evening lecture now. Sorry, have to fly."

As he climbed into his car, there was only one thing on his mind — Anneka. She'd had to look after her grandmother for the past three days, and he hadn't seen her. He'd missed her badly, and need-less to say was so horny he could barely think, but that would soon be remedied. She'd made a booking at a Frankston Motel, and he was tingling with excitement about what the night might hold. The drive along Beach Road was pleasant with the ocean on his right and grand, predominantly two-story houses on the other side. His mom was right; he was falling behind with his studies but what could he do? There were only so many hours in the week, and he had to keep up his casual work, or he wouldn't be able to afford to take Anneka out. He spent every minute he could with her, and when he didn't see her for a few days, it was sheer hell. He'd mentioned to her that he was struggling with his studies, and she'd suggested that they only see each other on weekends. That would give him the time he was looking for. He wouldn't hear of it. Then she had said that she might have something else that would help him.

When Raj George had met the despicable Douglas Aspine at his brother in law's funeral ten years earlier, he'd just been described in the media as Singapore's newest billionaire. He'd built on that and was now one of a handful of tycoons with enormous influence over the way Singapore was governed. He had been furious when Aspine had escaped from Changi and worried about his sister, Jasmine, knowing that Aspine was the type of snake who would seek revenge. Such was his fury, he had summoned the Police Commissioner and Prison Warden to his office, promising them if Aspine was not recaptured, he would have their jobs, a threat that he'd since carried out. Not only had he had arranged for security guards to watch Jasmine twenty-four hours a day, but he'd also beefed up the security around his own palatial mansion despite already having ten full-time servants. Nearly six months had elapsed since Aspine's escape, and nothing untoward had occurred, so Raj determined that it was time to call off the additional security. The last thing he wanted was for his concerns to unsettle or scare his sister. Besides, it was highly improbable that Douglas Aspine would ever set foot in Australia or Singapore again, and it was more likely that he was hiding out in South America.

Mick McHugh kept Aspine up to date at their weekly lunches at the Birmingham Hotel, which also seemed to pass for his office. He was big, loud and gregarious. Aspine enjoyed his company but was also wary of him. They were having a drink when his men had dragged this poor punter into the bar.

"Johnny." McHugh grinned. "Why have you been avoiding me?"

"I-I'll get you your money, Mick. Ya know I'm good for it."

"Money? I didn't even ask for my money, and here you are raising it. That's not the first thing mates talk about," McHugh said, resting his beer on the windowsill before clamping one hand over Johnny's mouth and grasping his nuts with the other. "But now you've raised it you little fucker, did ya really think ya were gonna do me outta five gorillas and still be capable of walking?"

McHugh released his hand ever so slightly from the terrified man's mouth, and he whimpered. "I-I'll ge-get it by thi-this Friday."

"Yeah, ya will, but it's now ten with the late payment charges."

"Tha-that's doub-double, and I only borrowed three grand to start wi-with."

"You're not objecting to my terms are ya?" McHugh snarled, tightening his grip.

"No-no," Johnny squealed, eyes rolling and sweat pouring from his forehead. "I'll have your money this Friday. I promise."

"Now that wasn't so hard, was it?" McHugh smiled, tightening his hand over Johnny's mouth while momentarily releasing his testicles and then with no warning crushing them with every ounce of his strength. As Johnny slumped to the floor unconscious, McHugh looked over to his men. "Get this piece of shit out of my sight," and then as if nothing had occurred said to Aspine, "Have ya decided what yer eating yet?"

After they'd finished their meals, Aspine said, "You charged that poor bastard seven grand in interest on a three thousand loan. How long was it for?"

"Not that it's any of your business, but it wasn't seven! It was two in interest and a late payment penalty fee of five. The loan was for six weeks."

"I'm not ever borrowing money off you." Aspine laughed.

"Are you gonna keep talking about that fucking loser or do you wanna know what's happening? I've only got so much time, you know."

"Sorry. Tell me where we're up to with that bitch, Jeczik, and the other whore's son?"

McHugh pushed himself back in his chair and put his feet up on the window ledge. "Those documents cost a bloody fortune, and I gotta tell you they're perfect."

Aspine hated the way McHugh talked about cost as if he were the one who was actually paying. McHugh also liked to claim credit for the plans much to Aspine's annoyance when he was just a tool to put them into action. However, after seeing what had happened to Johnny, Aspine wasn't about to complain.

"How do you know that, Mick? We won't know that until the bitch starts tearing Elmhurst apart on national television, and before that happens, she's going to have to take the bait."

"How do I know?" McHugh said. "Because I own a firm of accountants and a firm of lawyers and they've checked every document with a fine-tooth comb. Christ, they even advised the forgers."

Aspine burst out in raucous laughter. "Mick, that's crap, and you know it. You're not allowed to own firms of lawyers and accountants."

"For a guy who used to run a big public company you are one fucking dumbass," McHugh said, draining his beer and burping loudly. "Who do ya think the embezzlers, the fraudsters, and the white-collar crooks work for when they come out of prison? They're debarred, and can't get jobs other than flipping burgers, so they work for me."

"But they're not allowed to practice."

"Yeah, but they can for me." McHugh laughed. "You're not the only client of mine who I've helped out with a bitta professional advice. These guys are brilliant, and I've got 'em working sixty hours a week. Occasionally I need a practicing lawyer, but when I do, I get these guys to complete the brief, and then I take it along to one of the blue-blood firms and pay 'em a few grand to stick their name on it."

"Far out," Aspine said. "You amaze me. You're an underworld entrepreneur."

"You'd be staggered if ya knew the size of my empire." McHugh beamed, beckoning the barman to bring him another beer. "Now let me tell ya about Candy and young Jack Bartlett."

"Go on."

"He's head over heels in love with her. He'd never had sex before, and now he's fucking himself stupid. Candy's got him on Ecstasy, and she's about to introduce him to ice."

"I hate drugs." Aspine grimaced. "I actually feel for the kid, but his slut of a mom planted heroin on me, and she's gonna pay for her treachery in spades."

McHugh passed Aspine a photo. "Good looking girl, ain't she?"

"She's stunning but only young. Where'd you dig her up from?"

"She's actually twenty-four, though she could also pass for sixteen with a bit of makeup. That makes her versatile, and I gotta tell ya, very expensive."

Aspine groaned.

"What'd ya say?"

"Nothing, I yawned."

"She's the star property at my main escort agency, The Executive Suite."

"Fuck, you're into brothels as well. What pie don't you have a finger in?"

"Not brothels," McHugh growled. "Escort agencies and the girls are escorts. We never say brothel or prostitute. Candy's smart, and in a good week, she can earn twenty grand tax-free and still take the weekend off. And get this, she wouldn't see more than five clients. She's the crème de la crème of her profession, and that's why I gotta charge ya so much. Speaking of charges, ya better transfer another two hundred big ones into my account."

"Jesus, that's nearly a mil so far. When's the meter going to stop ticking?"

"If ya want the best ya gotta pay." McHugh smirked, burping loudly. "When this is over, I might even treat ya to a night with Candy, and it'll be on me."

"That's real generous, Mick. What do I get if I spend another mil? A set of steak knives?"

Chapter 31

JACK HAD NEVER HAD dinner at the Hyatt before, let alone stayed there. "This must have cost you a fortune," he said, picking at his steak. "What happened? Did you win the lottery or something?"

"I saved up because tonight is special. It's our three-month anniversary, and I wanted to do something special." Anneka smiled, squeezing Jack's hand. "Do you like it?"

"The food's great, but I'm uncomfortable with you paying, and especially when it's so expensive."

"Let's not spoil it by talking about money, darling. Just relax and enjoy yourself."

"I wish I could. My mom's been on my back about not attending lectures and falling behind with my studies. Oh, and she's becoming more insistent about meeting you," Jack said, hanging his head.

Anneka had known he would change and hadn't been surprised when he'd gone from being cheery and carefree to sullen and moody. Ecstasy does that. "I have something that will fix your university problems and put you right back on track." she smiled. "And I'd love to meet your mom, but I just need a little more time. You're the first serious boyfriend I've had, and I've never done the meet-the-parents' thing before. Come on, hon, cheer up. We're going to have a great time tonight."

"Okay, I've just been stressed and falling further behind. I need another six hours in the day. Whatever you have isn't going to give me that."

"You might be surprised. Come on, finish your wine. I'm dying to see what the rooms in this place are like."

The lift whooshed them to the fourteenth floor, and Anneka swiped her key card in 1412 to reveal a double bed, a minibar, a table, work desk and television. "Hmmph, it's no different to any other motel room," she said, as she wandered around. "Ooh, the bathroom's very nice though, and there's even a phone next to the loo."

"It's fine," Jack said, without enthusiasm.

"Who talks on the phone when they're sitting on the loo? Yuk." Anneka giggled, flopping on the bed. "Come and give me a cuddle, darling."

"Give me a minute or two," Jack said, sitting down at the desk. "I just feel so down and can't snap out of it. I wonder if I'm coming down with something."

"I'll fix that and your study problems," Anneka said, jumping off the bed and taking a small phial from her handbag. She tipped some of its white powdery contents onto a magazine cover. "Sniff this."

"What is it? It's not cocaine, is it? I'm not sniffing that shit."

"Of course it's not cocaine, silly. Trust me, you'll feel good, and it will work wonders for your endurance."

Jack put his nose to the magazine cover, took a deep breath and recoiled at the burning sensation in his nostrils. "Fuck. What is this shit?" Before he could finish, he felt the rush, and suddenly he was clear headed, sharp and had gone from feeling down to being on top of the world. His cock that had been limp only a minute before was throbbing and being strangled by his jeans and he tore them off. "Get on the bed," he gasped.

They never slept, and for the first time Jack could control and delay his orgasms. Even after his orgasm, his penis remained rock hard. Sex with Anneka had always been mind-blowing, but the white powder she had fed him, took him to a new dimension. When they checked out in the morning, he wasn't tired in the slightest and was totally focused. He'd never been that confident with Anneka, mesmerized by her beauty and wondering what she saw in him. Now he was self-assured, assertive and in control — the world was a wonderful place.

"What was that stuff you gave me last night?"

"Crystal meth, it's great for your stamina, clears your head and intensifies your focus. And best of all, you can control it," She lied.

"So, it's not addictive like cocaine?"

"It can be, but not if you're strong and only take it when you have to."

"Where'd you get it from?"

"You can get anything on campus if you know the right people." She laughed. "I'm sure you could get it on Melbourne's campus."

"You're right, I probably could." Jack grinned, exuding confidence he'd never felt before.

Anneka said she had to look after her grandmother that night, so Jack arrived home early on Sunday evening determined to get a few hours study out of the way. Before starting he Googled crystal meth and was shocked when most of the sites included *ice* in their name or content. He hadn't known what ice was, but he knew its effects from the many newspaper articles, usually about young men in fatal car accidents or committing murders in insane rages. There was a big difference between him and them though — they were addicts whereas he would only use it occasionally when he was tired and flat.

Besides, Anneka had told him that he'd be able to control his usage and she wouldn't lie. He felt great. Twelve hours later he was still in front of his computer having managed to put a huge dent in the backlog of work that he'd let pile up. Staggeringly, he still wasn't tired despite not having slept for forty-eight hours and nor was he hungry. He grabbed a glass of milk, jumped in his car and headed off to lectures. The finely ground white powder had given him the extra hours he was looking for.

By the end of the day, the euphoria finally wore off, and while Jack still wasn't tired, he was grumpy and irritable. He snapped at his younger brother, Sam, and when Jasmine told him to apologize, he stormed off to his room, slamming the door behind him.

"Maybe he had a fight with his girlfriend, Sam."

"He's strange, Mom. He's changed so much since he met Anneka and why doesn't he bring her home? Is he ashamed of us or something?"

"Don't be too hard on him. He's finding his way in the world. You might be the same when you find yourself a girlfriend." Jasmine laughed.

Chapter 32

SYDNEY TOWN HALL WAS packed with two thousand conservatives who'd come to pay homage to the Right Honorable William Elmhurst and celebrate his thirty years in Parliament. The stage curtain was drawn, and there was a buzz of anticipation emanating from the audience. Two beakers of water and half a dozen glasses sat on a small coffee table in the center of the stage with a leather recliner on either side of it. A large drape immediately behind the table was emblazoned with the Channel 16 logo. Strategically placed cameras took in every angle of the small area while others panned the audience. Gigantic overhead screens positioned on either side of the stage ensured that those sitting at the rear of the hall would not miss seeing and hearing the interview. Craig Chisholm was at the back of the stage chewing nervously on a piece of gum. Fiona's interview had been billed *An Evening with William Elmhurst* and would be beamed into the homes of a national audience. Fiona had ambushed many crooked politicians and businessmen over the years, but never quite like this. Lifelong friends of Elmhurst had been invited as had many members of his family.

Craig had been unable to prove that the documents were one hundred percent authentic and had asked Fiona to tread carefully. "Don't be aggressive until you're certain he's being evasive or lying. You'll be able to read his face and his emotions." She had promised she would be careful, but the patronizing tone of her voice suggested otherwise.

The curtains opened to loud applause to reveal Fiona dressed in a smart beige pants suit sitting opposite William Elmhurst who looked distinguished in a tailored three-piece charcoal gray suit. "William Elmhurst. Firstly, let me congratulate you for surviving and might I say thriving for thirty years in the bear pit that is the New South Wales lower house. What motivated you to go into politics as a young man?"

"Thank you, Fiona. There is no greater calling in life than serving the public. I felt that when I was a wet behind the ears backbencher, and I still feel it as a minister and elder statesman of the party."

"You've always been passionate about educating the young, and you're often described as the father of education. That must be gratifying."

"You're kind, but I don't know that that's true. There have been many fine politicians from both sides of politics in our great state who have made meaningful contributions to education."

"Yes, but under your stewardship funding for education has increased by fifty percent and the average class size is only twenty-two. There are those who say that it was grateful parents that won the Liberal party the last election. That must make you proud. Have you ever thought of running for premier?"

"We already have a fine premier and the education portfolio is very fulfilling," Elmhurst responded, taking a long sip of water. The questions and comments were identical to those that had been provided to his office.

"You have an impeccable record. You've never been investigated or been involved in any personal or political scandals. This would be remarkable in any jurisdiction, but more so in New South Wales which has a history of corruption stretching back over two hundred years to the first fleet. What made you so different from many of your peers? Was it because you came from a wealthy and privileged background and never wanted for anything?"

"You make me sound like a spoiled brat." Elmhurst laughed. "I came from a family of eight, and we were all taught the work ethic from an early age. I sold newspapers and worked in a milk bar to put myself through university. Yes, my parents were wealthy, but I never saw them pull a fast deal or take advantage of anyone who'd fallen on hard times. I think honesty is learned by example and I had two of the finest examples that our good Lord has ever created. Bless their souls."

"Amen," Fiona said. "I'm sorry, but we have to take a short ad break. We could not air programs like this without our advertisers."

As Fiona got up to stretch her legs, Craig took her by the arm. "I need to see you."

"Not now, we're back on in less than three minutes."

"Yes, now," Craig said, leading her to the back of the stage. "I've been watching Elmhurst. He's too calm. He knows your reputation, and he would've seen you tear other guests to pieces, and yet he's not worried. I have a terrible feeling about this, Fiona. Please drop it. You can fill in for another forty minutes and make it the feel-good interview his supporters are expecting."

"You've totally misread him, Craig. I've lulled him into a false sense of security because he thinks he's going to get the questions we forwarded to his office. Well, he's about to get a rude awakening, and I'm going to serve him up to those *born to rule* sycophants who are here to cheer him on," Fiona snapped. "Don't interrupt me again."

"For God's sake, be careful. He's not like the others. He's survived three decades in the toughest and dirtiest political forum there is, and he's come out unscathed."

Fiona strode back to her chair listening to one of the production crew going through the timing cues.

"Ten seconds, five seconds, one second and we're on."

Douglas Aspine sat in the back row of the hall gloating. The bitch had set him up before, and he'd watched her do the same to countless others. Now she was about to lower the boom on one of the most highly respected, almost revered, politicians in the land.

"Your family has vast pastoral and cattle interests in New South Wales. Tell me about the acreage you have in Gunnedah."

"Unfortunately, we never owned any land in Gunnedah. What we did own was further west, and the ground was like concrete. It wasn't fit for dingoes." Elmhurst laughed.

"So, you sold it?"

"Yes, we disposed of it."

"I'm sorry." Fiona smiled. "Is there a difference between selling and disposing of?"

"In terms of ownership and the title, no," Elmhurst responded, crossing his ankles and leaning back into his recliner.

"I'll make it simple for you. Did you or your family receive monies or any other consideration on disposal?"

"It was a long time ago. I really can't remember the details."

"Would it surprise you to know that when you disposed of that barren land, it was incredibly valuable, and sitting atop millions of tons of thermal coal?"

"No, that's not true. The land wasn't valuable. It only became valuable when an exploration license and development permits were issued a few years later."

Fiona could hardly believe her luck. Elmhurst was admitting the actions he took in the New South Wales Parliament had led to a vast increase in the value of the land. "So, you didn't know about the coal when you disposed of the land?"

"Of course we did. Half the land in New South Wales has coal below the surface, but if it can't be mined, it has no value. Our family are farmers, not miners. With respect, what does this have to with my political career or portfolio?"

"Just a few more questions," Fiona responded. "Does the name Benefish Proprietary Limited mean anything to you?"

"Vaguely. Should it?"

"It's the company that you disposed of the land to. Do you, your family or any entity associated with you have an interest in this company or any trust related to it?"

Finally, the penny dropped and Elmhurst's lips closed to form a single thin line. "I'd be careful if I were you, Ms. Jeczik."

"Would you be surprised if I told you that one of your accountant's nominee companies owns half the shares in Benefish Proprietary Limited and a nominee company of your lawyers owns the other half? In effect, you disposed of the land to yourself, and some four years later used your position in the New South Wales parliament to ensure licenses and permits were issued that would add greatly to its value," Fiona said, her bottom lip curled up in disgust.

A shocked murmur went through the hall, and Elmhurst sat forward, red-faced and clutched his hands together. "That is a blatant lie and totally defamatory."

"Didn't Benefish Proprietary Limited then sell the land to Clean

Coal Limited for shares in that company? Shares that are now worth two hundred million dollars and on which your son has derived millions in dividends."

Elmhurst's glasses had slipped down his nose, and his eyes were red and angry as he stared at Fiona over the top of the frame. "My family and I have had no interest in the land since it was disposed of. I don't know where you got your information from, but it's wrong."

"That's what you'd like us to th–"

"Enough," Elmhurst said, jumping up from his recliner. "I'll not listen to any more of this. You'll be hearing from my lawyers in the morning."

The audience was shocked, and some started booing and catcalling Fiona. Others filed out of the hall looking at their feet. Some were glued to their chairs, totally stunned. Douglas Aspine bounced out of the door with a spring in his step.

The first person who Fiona caught sight of was Craig. "I told you he was a crooked bastard," she said. "Did you see him squirming?"

"No, but I heard him instructing his lawyers. He was furious, and there wouldn't have been anyone backstage who didn't hear him."

"Craig, how many legal threats have been made against me that have ever amounted to anything? None, zippo, zilch." Fiona laughed. "He's just like the rest of those crooks, all hot air. Did you see the stunned faces of his disciples?"

Craig knew it was no good arguing. Fiona would be on a high for hours — she always was when she brought some big-shot down and the more powerful they were, the bigger the buzz. The Right Honorable William Elmhurst was about as big as they came.

Chapter 33

DOUGLAS ASPINE WAS WORRIED. He'd been out of prison for over six months and still hadn't had sex. Nor had he had any strong desire. Perhaps prison and a diet of bromide did that. Or could it be that age had sexually caught up with him? He'd put on ten kilograms, was toned from working out in the gym, and actually liked what he saw in the mirror other than for two massive love handles. Why Sonchai hadn't got rid of them when he removed the superfluous stomach skin was beyond Aspine — on reflection it really wasn't, and one thing Sonchai never did was freebies.

When I leave Australia for one of those South American republics, I'll have to take a circuitous route via Bangkok and make one last visit to Sonchai.

Many times, he'd thought about asking Mick McHugh to organize a girl from one of his escort agencies, but then fear had taken over. What if he couldn't perform and the girl blabbed? He would be a laughing stock, and he'd already seen McHugh's cruel side.

It had just gone 10 P.M. when he arrived home from the Elmhurst interview on a huge high, and he needed to celebrate with more than booze. There were plenty of Melbourne escort agencies listed on the net, and Aspine called the appropriately named Desperate Desires and told the receptionist specifically what he was looking for. Thirty minutes later he heard his front door buzzer and when he answered a statuesque, olive skinned brunette in her mid-thirties smiled at him. "Hi, Mr. Adderley, I'm Ramona from the agency."

Aspine liked what he saw. *If I can't get it up for you, I'll never get it up.* "Come in, it's Charles," he said. "Would you like a drink?"

"Let's get the business out of the way first. It's a thousand, and if you want anything kinky like a golden shower or anal, it'll be more."

"I'm not a fucking weirdo," Aspine growled, handing Ramona a fistful of notes. "It's all there."

"I'm sure it is," she said, carefully counting it. "Why don't we adjourn to the bedroom? You can make yourself comfortable while I undress."

A few minutes later she was down to a matching black lace bra, G-string, and stilettoes. She slunk over to the bed like a cat and began slowly unbuttoning Aspine's shirt while running her hands up and down his chest. Nothing was happening, and he wondered whether prison had made him impotent. It certainly wasn't Ramona because she was stunning, and in one swift movement she unclipped her bra and placed his hands on her full brown breasts. Recoiling, she said, "What's wrong with your hands?" and pushed him away.

"I had an accident," he grunted. "They were crushed in a machine."

"God, they felt like sandpaper on my boobs." She giggled, examining his hands before placing them back on her breasts. "That was an unexpected shock. Be gentle."

"Yeah, yeah," he growled, more concerned that her incredible body and looks were having no effect.

"Relax," she said, unbuckling his belt and pulling down his fly. "Hmmm, what do we have here? Don't tell me Roger doesn't want to come out to play."

Aspine's worst fear had been being unable able to respond to a beautiful, sexy woman, and Ramona was working overtime with her hands around his penis, and nothing was happening. "I can't give you head without a condom, and I don't think we could get one on," she murmured.

Fuck! Why is nothing happening? For no reason, his mind wandered to the arrest of Sir Edwin Philby, and he felt a stirring.

"Roger's a big boy." Ramona laughed, flicking off her G-string. "My touch has never been known to fail."

"Quick," said Aspine, fearing his erection wouldn't last. It had been ten years, and he tried in vain to control the speed of his thrusting before letting out an almighty scream as he orgasmed.

"Jesus, when was the last time you had sex?"

Aspine didn't answer. "You can leave now."

"You've still got another forty minutes, and maybe Roger will rise to the occasion again."

"Get dressed and get the fuck out of here."

"All right, all right, I'm going, and you said you weren't a weirdo. Bullshit."

"Don't make me angry." Aspine threatened.

He was happy. He wasn't impotent. Stress used to turn him on, but now it was the thought of wreaking revenge on his enemies. *I suppose I should be thankful that I can still make it stand up.*

Every major morning newspaper across the nation headlined the fraud the supposedly squeaky-clean William Elmhurst had perpetrated. Television breakfast programs replayed excerpts of the interviews ad nauseam, and serious faced political commentators said that it could bring the government down. Radio talkback hosts were outraged, and ferals screamed for Elmhurst to be jailed. Others attacked the Independent Commission against Corruption for going to sleep at the wheel. Vicious as these attacks were, they paled into insignificance with what Elmhurst was called in meeting rooms and blogs on the net. Attempts to contact the member met without success, the only comment from his office was that he had instructed his lawyers to commence action against Channel 16 and Fiona Jeczik and that he would make a statement to the parliament that evening.

Lawyers at Hedgewick & Carson, the largest of the law firms that the Elmhurst family used had worked through the night and at precisely 2 P.M. the following day served bulky defamation writs and statements of claim on Channel 16 and Fiona Jeczik. While the speed of the action was unusual, the actual serving of the defamation writs had occurred many times before and was something that all major media organizations were subject to. Accordingly, the writs and supporting documents were couriered to Channel 16's lawyers, Barbour & Arnold, who before the day was out would most likely tell the learned brethren at Hedgewick & Carson to fuck off, charging eight hundred dollars an hour to do so, and using gentrified legalese as opposed to mere street crudities.

At 5 P.M. the senior partner at Hedgewick & Carson called his counterpart at Barbour & Arnold. They had gone through university together, regularly saw each other socially and were members of the Melbourne Club and Royal Melbourne Golf Club. Fifteen minutes later the senior partner of Barbour & Arnold felt ill, knowing that there was no defense against the action and that his clients had wantonly and viciously defamed the Right Honorable William Elmhurst. Telling aggressive clients that they had been wrong and that their actions were indefensible was never easy.

The New South Wales parliament was hushed, and the press and public galleries were overflowing when William Elmhurst rose to speak. He spoke eloquently and told of his family's desire for privacy when they made gifts to charitable institutions, and that was why he had used the words disposed of in relation to the Gunnedah land. The family had not sold the land but gifted it to Benefish Proprietary Limited as trustee of a trust with ten specific public charitable institutions as beneficiaries including The Anti-Cancer Council, Sydney Children's Hospital and Seeing Eye Dogs Australia. Other than the tax deduction for the gift, the family had not derived any benefit from its largesse. Accordingly, when Elmhurst had voted on the exploration license and development permit, neither he nor his family derived any financial benefit and had had no involvement in the subsequent sale to Clean Coal Limited. Fortunately, Clean Coal Limited had been very successful, and the dividends it had paid to Benefish Proprietary Limited had found their way to needy charities. The lawyers and accountants who had advised on the gift and managed the trust provided their services *pro bono* thus maximizing charitable distributions. It should have been a *feel-good* story, but somehow Channel 16 and its star performer had managed to turn it into something sordid and unsavory.

"Those who have defamed my family and me, including those who blindly followed Channel 16 in this morning's media, will feel the full weight of the law," Elmhurst thundered. "Writs have already been issued, and many more will follow. I am a very private person, and I seek no accolades for the gifts and donations that my family and I make. Accordingly, revealing what I have today is not something I would normally do. Unfortunately, given the circumstances, I had no choice. Thank you for hearing me out."

As Elmhurst took his seat, members from both sides of the house stood and applauded and were quickly followed by those in the public gallery. It was only those in the press gallery and Craig Chisholm who remained seated and glum-faced.

Craig had taken a midday flight to Sydney specifically to listen to Elmhurst's statement and had sat in the tightly packed public gallery. By the time it was over, he was trembling and wrought with emotion. He had warned Fiona but knew it wouldn't save him or the rest of the team, and that they would all be on the scrapheap before the week was out. What was the purpose of the setup? Did someone hate Elmhurst so much that they would go to enormous trouble and expense to bring him down? Or was it Fiona they were after and Elmhurst was just a pawn they used to get to her? Whoever engineered the setup was extremely cunning and not lacking financial resources. If the target was Fiona, one name came immediately to mind.

Chapter 34

JACK BARTLETT WAS SNORTING ice at least twice a week but still telling himself that he had it under control. He hardly needed sleep anymore, his work output was prodigious, and making love to Anneka was totally mind-blowing, and even better when she sniffed as well. She would prepare two lines usually on magazine covers, but unbeknown to Jack would tip nearly all of hers back into the phial, only imbibing just a few grains. She had seen what ice had done to others and had no intention of becoming a drug addict.

It was about ten weeks after sniffing his first line when Jack waited for Anneka in a small St Kilda coffee shop. He was annoyed and irritable and getting sick of her coming up with lame excuses not to meet his mom and brother. She was running late, and Jack tapped his feet and wrung his hands impatiently. *Where the bloody hell was she?* A few minutes later she sat down gently kissing him on the lips. "You're late," he snarled.

"Honey, settle down. It took me ages to find a park. I'm five minutes late."

"You should've left home earlier. I can't fucking stand tardiness."

"I'm sorry, is there anything I can do to make it up to you?"

"Have you got any stuff on you?"

"Of course. I wouldn't let my lover down. Are you feeling run down?"

"Pass it under the table, and I'll go to the toilet." *Why won't she stop talking?*

When Jack returned he was smiling, confident and happy, the anger and impatience that he'd been experiencing only a few minutes earlier had vanished. "You know you get an even bigger rush when you inject," Anneka said.

"Inject? I'm not injecting. Not ever. I'm no bloody druggie, and that's what druggies do. Come on, let's get out of here and find a cheap motel. I want to spend the rest of the day fucking you."

Anneka knew that he was almost hooked. Three months ago, he would have never used words like that, the closest being that he was in love and dying to make love to her. "Okay, you sure are frisky." She giggled.

"You better believe it, babe. I'm gonna ride you all the way to Texas."

Barry Seymour, Channel 16's CEO, sat gloomily behind his desk staring out at Port Phillip Bay's choppy green and blue hues. "You wanted to see me," Fiona said, taking a seat opposite him.

"Yes, I think you know why."

"How bad is it?"

"Elmhurst's lawyers are demanding separate full-page apologies from us, and you personally in all the national dailies. In addition, they've demanded that the lead story in our national news tonight is a *mea culpa* confessing to the public that we stuffed up. Jesus, Fiona, how could you go to air with a half-assed story like that? What's wrong with Craig Chisholm? It's his job to make sure that stuff-ups like this never occur."

"It wasn't Craig's fault. He warned me, but I overrode him. What else do Elmhurst's lawyers want?"

"Five million in damages payable as a donation to the Children's Leukemia & Cancer Foundation."

"Jeez, are you going to pay?"

"What choice do we have? If we don't, the litigation will drag on for years, and instead of reporting the news, we'll be the news. The board decided earlier today that we needed to nip it in the bud and put the whole sorry debacle behind us."

"I wasn't told about any board meeting," Fiona said, raising her eyebrows.

"Fiona, the board determined not to continue with your services and accepted your resignation as a director. You can spend the rest of the day cleaning out your office and packing your personal belongings."

"I never resigned!"

"No, but I told them you had. They wanted to call an extraordinary general meeting and hang you out to dry in public. I didn't think that would help you or us."

"Did any of them support me?"

"Not one. If it makes you feel better, they considered my position as well. They're angry, and we've had advertisers threatening to take their business elsewhere unless you were fired."

"I made this channel," Fiona said, fighting back the tears of anger. "You would've never had those advertisers without my investigative journalism."

"That might be true, but no one in this business remembers the good things; everyone remembers the bad. They'll still be talking about the Elmhurst interview in twenty years' time, and budding journalists will probably study it. Fiona, you have a chip on your shoulder that clouds your judgment when it comes to those you see as privileged, because Rupert Murdoch fired your father. That was progress and typesetters were simply replaced by computers. If Murdoch hadn't moved with the times, he wouldn't be in business today. You might just as well have assassinated Mother Teresa as accuse Elmhurst without watertight evidence. What were you thinking?"

Fiona didn't agree but saw no point in arguing. "Did William Elmhurst apply pressure to have me sacked?"

"No. His office said we should do what good corporate governance called for, but we were not to read that as a call for your dismissal."

"He is a good man, but someone hates him enough to go to a lot of trouble to bring him down." Fiona sniffled.

"Or you?" Seymour said.

"Don't think I haven't thought of that. There's only one person I can think of who's that hateful and has the brains and money to pull it off — Douglas Aspine. Craig drew the same conclusion, but when you think about it, there's no way he'd run the risk of coming back to Australia, and I doubt he could have orchestrated it from overseas."

"First it was Mary Denton, then Sir Edwin Philby and now you. It seems to be stretching coincidence to its limit. I can feel his evil hands all over this."

"Yes, but there's one huge flaw in that theory. Surely Jasmine

Bartlett would be the first person he would have gone after. After all, she was the one who framed him and put him away for twenty years."

"Hmmm, perhaps."

"Barry, what am I going to do? Channel 16 has been the whole of my life. I don't know anything else other than television, and I'm hardly likely to be snapped up by another channel."

"I'll give you the same advice I gave Craig. Your termination package is extremely generous. Take a sabbatical, go overseas for a year, and when you come back, I might be able to do something for you."

"What? You've sacked Craig too? That's so unfair. I told you he warned me not to try and take Elmhurst down. He's not at fault," Fiona railed.

"Fiona, he's been your producer since day dot. You're joined at the hip. With you gone we need a totally new approach to the news and current affairs. If it's any comfort, Craig said that without you, he would've resigned anyway. He was happy getting sacked knowing how much extra cash it put in his pocket." Seymour laughed, as he got up and cuddled her. "I'll miss you."

"Me too," she gulped.

Chapter 35

BILL MULLER SPREAD THE morning newspapers out on his kitchen table. In direct contrast to the prior day, every front page carried a headline about how William Elmhurst had been defamed. The articles were savage and accused Fiona Jeczik of sloppy journalism. Many critics hypocritically claimed she had brought the whole profession into disrepute. Usually, when the media made mistakes, apologies were hidden in the back pages of the dailies, but this wasn't the case with Channel 16 and Fiona. Most of the papers carried prominent double page spreads headed: *Apologies to the Right Honorable William Elmhurst.* Many carried their own smaller retractions, not leaving out the fact that the stories they had printed had originated from being misled by Fiona Jeczik. All of them carried stories about Channel 16 donating five million dollars to the Children's Leukemia & Cancer Foundation. While Elmhurst's office claimed no credit for this, the reporters were quick to praise him. The financial pages covered the ten percent fall in Channel 16's share price and Fiona's sudden resignation from the board. The more pointed articles said that it was obvious she'd been given a choice *resign, or we'll fire you.*

Muller read every word and when he'd finished made himself a strong black coffee and sat down in his thinking chair. He hadn't believed it, but what had occurred with Mary Denton and Sir Edwin Philby may just have been coincidence, but the debacle that had befallen Fiona Jeczik completely destroyed the coincidence theory. The people who had helped destroy Douglas Aspine were getting their comeuppance, and it wasn't happening by chance. Muller flicked his Teledex open to J and called Fiona on her cell phone. She had no hesitation in agreeing to meet him in the city for coffee at midday. Muller didn't put the phone down. Instead, he worked it for the next two hours calling cops and ex-crims looking for a lead.

The Paris End Café was small, and on a nice day, the few tables on Collins Street were popular. The phone calls had made Muller late, and he was huffing and puffing as he approached the café. He could see Fiona and a man he recognized as one of her associates sitting at one of the street tables. She had been the face of national television, and curious passersby slowed to get a better look at her. "This is like a reunion," Muller said, extending his hand to Fiona.

She put her cup down. "You remember my producer, Craig Chisholm. Oops, make that former producer."

"G'day, Craig," Muller said, looking around for a waitress, "Latte, thanks love."

"I never expected to see you again," Fiona said. "You haven't changed a bit." *You looked sixty and carried a lot of lines ten years ago, Bill, and you still look sixty and have the same lines.*

"Likewise, but that was before our old friend reappeared."

"What?" Craig said. "Have you discovered he's back?"

"No such luck, but I had a hunch, and after what happened to Fiona, I'm fairly sure he's pulling the strings."

"Perhaps, but what if the misinformation was to hurt William Elmhurst, and that I was just collateral damage?" Fiona said.

"Hurt William Elmhurst?" Muller laughed. "Thanks to you he's the most popular politician in Australia. The conservatives were going to get thrashed at the next election, and now they're six points in front. If Elmhurst was inclined, he could challenge the premier and romp in. He won't because he's too loyal. You didn't hurt him; you made him a bloody saint."

"It's hard to argue against that logic," Fiona said, glancing at Craig.

"It's black and white. Aspine escapes from Changi, Mary Denton gets charged with shoplifting, Sir Edwin Philby gets caught with kiddie porn, and you get lured into doing an interview that ruins your career. You don't really think that's coincidental, do you?"

"It's certainly persuasive, but why wouldn't he have gone after Jasmine Bartlett first?" Craig asked. "He must hate her more than anyone else."

"I don't know. I called her this morning and asked if anything different had recently occurred in her life. She responded in the negative and I didn't want to push it. I didn't want to scare her on the off chance that I might be wrong."

"You're like me with the Elmhurst interview." Fiona laughed. "You're ninety-nine percent sure."

"Do you think he's in Australia?" Craig asked.

"I don't know. I called all of my contacts, and one name kept popping up: Mick McHugh. There are only four forgers in Australia capable of producing the documents you got suckered with, and I was going to have a talk with them. However, if McHugh's involved, there's no way anyone's going to be talking."

"I checked the supposed Crime Commission offices in the T & G Building the morning after the interview. The elevators that wouldn't stop on level 10 now do, and there were *for lease* signs all over the place. It was a ploy to mislead us, and it worked perfectly. I'd already asked the agent who the tenant was and got nowhere. I thought once the space was vacant I'd try again. He wouldn't breathe a word, and I sensed he was scared. It fits with what you said about McHugh, but I have to say that surprises me because he doesn't seem all bad," Craig said. "He's often in the social pages, and he does a lot of good work for charities."

"Don't be fooled. He's gregarious and charming on the outside, but underneath the veneer, he's a cold-blooded killer. Police suspect him of committing at least ten homicides, but he's never had to spend a day in court defending himself. We had him stone cold on one murder charge. Then the star witness committed suicide, and others disappeared or suddenly found themselves suffering from amnesia."

"How would Aspine ever get to know someone like McHugh?" Fiona asked.

"He was in prison for nearly ten years, and he'd have contacts, and those contacts would have contacts. I guess that one of his Changi mates told him about McHugh."

"Okay, let's say that everything you claim is kosher," Fiona said. "How would Aspine have ever found out enough about William Elmhurst's personal business to put that scam together?"

"That's troubled me, too, but I think I have the answer. At his peak, Aspine was a powerful business figure dealing with the largest legal, accounting and stockbroking firms in the land. Let's say he over-heard something about Elmhurst that he wasn't meant to hear, and he tucked it away in his memory bank for a rainy day. Slime bags like Aspine are always on the lookout for leverage."

"Jesus, that's so bloody thin." Craig scoffed. "You were going so well, but that's a bridge too far."

"Loose lips sink ships." Muller grinned. "Yeah, I know it's lame, but my gut tells me I'm right."

"I think you're right, but I'm not sure it helps," Fiona said. "You told us that there are no loose lips around Mick McHugh, and we're not going to get anything out of his associates. So, what do we do?"

"We watch and stay in contact with Jasmine Bartlett, because if I'm right, Aspine's coming for her."

Chapter 36

JACK BARLETT RUSHED TO the bathroom, and dry retched into the toilet bowl. There was nothing to bring up because he hadn't eaten for days. He was angry with himself, angry with Anneka, angry with the world and when he looked in the mirror, he recoiled in horror. His eyes were yellow, and his teeth were black. He turned away, held his head in his hands and shook it, trying to control the demons that were tearing his brain apart. When he looked in the mirror again, his eyes had returned to their normal dark brown, and his teeth were white. He was seething when he returned to his room and let out an angry scream when he couldn't find his wallet.

"Sam, Sam, you little fucker. Give me my fucking wallet back. I'll fucking kill you."

Sam looked at his mother with palms uplifted. "I don't know what he's talking about."

"Don't you use language like that in this house," Jasmine shouted, banging loudly on Jack's door.

A bottle crashed into the door and smashed all over the floor. "He's gone mad, Mom. Don't go in there," Sam pleaded.

Jasmine pushed the door open, and Jack was standing, holding his desktop monitor over his head as if he was going to hurl it at her. "Put that down," she said. "Put it down now."

"I'll call the police, Mom," Sam said.

"No, Sam, Jack will be all right, won't you Jack? Now come on, please put the monitor down and then we can talk about what's troubling you."

As Jack lowered the monitor, Jasmine saw his wallet under his desk where he'd obviously dropped it, and she picked it up. "Here's your wallet," she said, handing it to him. "Apologize to your brother."

"Fuck him and fuck you," Jack yelled, seizing his wallet and storming out of the house.

"What's wrong with him, Mom?" Sam said. "He's changed so much. I don't think I know him anymore."

"He works and studies so hard," Jasmine said. "I think he needs a good long rest."

Jack sped out of his street and onto High Street Road just managing to stop behind two cars waiting for the lights to turn green. He was angry, impatient and desperate for a fix. *Why don't they go through the fucking red light?* He hit the horn while revving the guts out his car. When the lights turned, he flew past the two cars giving their drivers the finger. Desperate, he called Anneka, "I need to see you," he yelled. "I need ice."

"I can't get out tonight," She lied. "I'm looking after granny."

"Fuck granny. Don't you understand? I'm going through hell?"

"Where are you?"

"In the car park in St Kilda where we always meet. Hurry, I can't last much longer."

"I'll be there as quick as I can, but I can't stay, I have to get back home."

"Just bring the stuff and fucking hurry up," Jack screamed.

Thirty minutes later Anneka pulled into the dark car park overlooking the bay and parked next to Jack. "Give it to me. Give it to me," he yelled. She handed him a phial, and he tipped the contents on his bonnet. Taking huge breaths, he snorted what would have been four lines, and a few minutes later his head was clear. He was no longer angry or impatient, he felt great.

"I'm horny. Let's jump in the back seat."

"I told you I have to get back home. I can't."

"Fuck you," he snarled, anger surging through him again.

"I'm sorry. I wish I could, honey. You know that."

"Just a quickie then," he said, giving her his best charming boyish smile.

"Jack, I have to go. We can fool around at the weekend."

"All right, fuck off then. I don't need you to get laid."

As Anneka drove away, she knew her job was done, that she'd never see or hear from Jack Bartlett again. He was totally hooked, his face had a distinct meth rash from where he'd been scratching, and he was bipolar. Jack had been a nice kid, and she wasn't proud of what she had done, but Mick McHugh wasn't someone you refused. At least he'd be pleased when her supervisor called to tell him *mission complete*. When she got home, she would destroy the prepaid cell phone that Jack had contacted her on and delete her email address, removing all means by which he could contact her.

Chapter 37

IT WAS 9 A.M. WHEN Douglas Aspine read the small article at the bottom of page 17 of the *Herald Sun* and was infuriated. The police had dropped all charges against Sir Edwin Philby on the advice of the Director of Public Prosecutions that it was unlikely convictions would be attained. Aspine had always realized that this was a possibility but had hoped against hope that the charges would at least be heard in open court. It was the first setback he had suffered since escaping from Changi, and he tried to fight the pressure building in his temples to no avail. He put his hands on his forehead and gently tried to massage the stress away, but still, it continued to build. Almost without thinking he picked up his cell phone and punched in the number for Desperate Desires. "I need a girl," he barked.

"Mr. Adderley," the receptionist responded. "I'm sorry, if you're looking for Ramona, she doesn't start until midday."

"I don't care who you send," Aspine said, and then paused. "But don't send me anyone wearing a muzzle or she won't get in the door." *Fuck! I didn't say my name, but they've got all my details. They've obviously recorded my phone number. I better get a new prepaid.*

"I'm sure you'll be pleased with Felicity. She's a blue-eyed blonde with–"

"She'll do," Aspine cut in.

Felicity was an attractive, petite blonde with a cheery smile and a silicon enhanced upper deck. She normally spent fifteen minutes talking to a new John before getting down to action, but when Douglas Aspine opened the front door, he was obviously aroused. He pushed five hundred dollars into her hand and said, "Get your clothes off and get into bed, I've got no time to waste."

She took no time at all and lay in bed watching him while he fought to pull down the jammed zip on his pants. "Do you need a hand?" She giggled.

Aspine didn't reply, finally releasing the zip and kicking his pants off. When he turned to face her, he was rolling a condom onto his fully erect penis. "My, my, you are frisky, aren't you? I don't get many early morning call outs."

He jumped into bed grasping her breasts roughly and climbing on in one movement. He made no attempt to control the speed or force of his thrusting and Felicity might just as well have been a piece of dead meat. Three minutes later he rolled off and threw the condom on the floor.

"Was that good?" she sniffled, disgusted by the feel of his hands.

"Get out."

"What?"

"Get dressed and fuck off. I've paid you, and you've served your purpose."

After Felicity had gone, Aspine lay on the bed staring at the ceiling, a huge smirk on his face. He'd had countless similar sexual experiences and afterward had always been disgusted with himself, but today he wasn't. He was relieved. *My equipment's functioning perfectly. I just needed a little stress to trigger it.*

Jack Bartlett's life was spiraling out of control. When he was home, he never left his bedroom or ate anything. He couldn't stand the sight of his mother or brother and was in a perpetual rage. When he called Anneka, he got a Telstra message telling him the service had been disconnected. When he called Telstra, they couldn't tell him why the service had been disconnected as it would breach privacy laws. Nor could they tell him if Anneka had a new service. His emails bounced and in desperation he had driven out to the huge Monash campus in Clayton, and drove around the car parks hoping to find her.

There were dents in every panel of his once immaculate car, but when Jasmine asked how they'd occurred, Jack had no idea and shouted at her to get off his back and leave him alone. Tantrums were the norm, and anything that could be smashed or thrown was. Jasmine and Sam were in fear of the madman who lived with them. Physically he was a bag of bones having lost more than ten kilograms, there were rashes on his face, and his eyes were dark and sunken. Mentally he was in the darkest of dark worlds.

Four days had passed since Jack had seen Anneka and he was beyond desperate. Impatience, anger and terrible hallucinations filled his life. He could neither eat nor sleep. The flashbacks and dreams drove him into another world where self-control did not exist. In wild frenzies, he smashed plates, cups, computer screens and windows but had no memory of doing so. The black dog would appear from nowhere and drive him to the depths of depression, and the thought of taking his life was ever present.

Jasmine was beside herself with worry when she called Bill Muller, the ex-policeman who had contacted her out of the blue prying about Douglas Aspine. She had wanted to meet him at a coffee shop, but he had kept her on the phone plying her with questions about what she wanted to see him about. In the end, she had broken down and told him everything. "Will you meet me? Can you help?"

"Yes, and I don't know. I need to see Jack, so there's no point meeting for coffee. I need to come to your home."

"What do you think it is?"

Muller knew exactly what it was. He'd served on the drug squad for more than ten years. What he didn't know was how bad it was. "I don't know," He lied. "I hope to be able to tell after I've seen Jack. Can I come over tonight?"

"Yes, yes, I suppose so. I can't guarantee that he'll be home. He has a girlfriend and comes and goes as he pleases, but he's been home the past few nights.

Chapter 38

IT WAS EARLY EVENING when Bill Muller pulled up out the
front of Jasmine Bartlett's weatherboard house in middle-class
Glen Iris. He stopped and ran his eye over an old blue Ford parked
in the driveway. It was filthy, and there were scrapes and dents all
over it. Empty bottles and food wrappers littered the inside. A piece
of plywood covered an obviously broken window at the rear of the
house. Parked three houses away on the street was a silver Toyota
Camry that Muller paid no attention to. Mick McHugh's man took
half a dozen pics of the ex-cop and texted them to his boss.

Jasmine was waiting on the front veranda. "Thank you for coming,
detective. Jack's been shouting and crashing around his room all day.
I think he's going mad."

She was frowning, and her eyes were red and puffy. "It's Bill, Mrs.
Bartlett, I'm no longer on the force."

"Sorry, I forgot, and please call me Jasmine. Can we talk out here?"
Jasmine asked as Sam joined them. "Sam, this is the man I told you
about, Mr. Muller."

"Hello, Sam." Muller grinned, more than happy for the boy to call
him Bill but not wanting to contradict Jasmine. "Can you tell me
when you first noticed changes in Jack?"

"About six months ago, but they were good changes," Sam replied.
"He'd just met Anneka, and was really happy. He was singing around
the house and even bought some new clothes."

"What's she like? Does she know what's troubling Jack?"

"We don't know. We've never met or spoken to her." Jasmine sighed.

"Hold on. You said Jack's been taking her out for six months. How
come you haven't met her?"

"He said that she was shy and that she wanted to meet us, but
needed time," Jasmine said.

140

"So, you've never even seen her," Muller said, shaking his head.

"Not in real life, but Jack showed me photos," Jasmine said. "She's stunning."

Jack texted me some photos when he first started taking her out," Sam said, taking out his cell phone. "He was so proud and wanted to show her off. Here look at these."

"She's attractive. Can you send those photos to me, Sam?"

"What does Anneka have to do with what Jack's going through?" Jasmine asked.

"Probably nothing. It's my police background. I like to cover all bases. When did you first start noticing changes for the worse?"

"Jack didn't really change, but he started to miss lectures and fall behind with his studies," Jasmine said. "He had part time jobs to fit in as well, and we didn't see him from Friday night until Monday morning. We guessed that he was spending weekends with Anneka. He was tired and a little stressed, but he didn't take it out on us. He was still our gentle, kind, loving Jack."

"About three months ago he started studying through the night and going to lectures the following morning," Sam said. "It was amazing, he seemed not to need sleep, and it wasn't long before he'd caught up with his studies. He became more intense, angry and moody but we just put it down to how hard he was working."

"And the anger gradually intensified," Muller said." He became impatient, snapped at you for making innocent everyday comments, and accused you of stealing when he couldn't find something. This morphed into rages, and he threatened to hurt or kill you. Then he started breaking and throwing things."

"Yes," Jasmine said. "How do you know?"

"I've seen it before, more times than I can count, and that's not the worst. He's suffering, and his life is a roller coaster of huge highs and terrible lows. Right now, he's in the depths of depression and needs help, desperately needs help."

"You didn't answer my question!"

Muller looked at his shoes before staring into Jasmine's eyes. "I hate to tell you, but Jack's a drug addict."

"No, no, that can't be true." Jasmine cried.

"I think he's right, Mom."

"I'm sorry, Jasmine, but if I'm going to help, I need to meet Jack," Muller said.

"Yes, yes," Jasmine whimpered. "Could he be...could he be suicidal?"

Her husband has taken his own life, and Muller could see the fear in her eyes. "We're going to help Jack," he said. "Let's go inside and talk to him."

Jasmine knocked gently on Jack's bedroom door. "Jack, can we come in? I have someone here who wants to talk to you."

"Leave me alone."

"We just want to help you, darling."

A glass or bottle smashed against the bedroom door. "Didn't you hear me? Leave me fucking well alone."

"He never used to swear," Jasmine whispered.

"Jack, my name's Bill Muller, and I'm coming in to talk to you whether you like it or not."

"You come in, and I'll fucking kill you."

"Maybe you should come back another time." Jasmine sniffled, fighting back the tears.

"No, let's get this over now," Muller said, shoving the door open.

Muller ducked to his left as a bottle whistled past his head and crashed into the wall. "Get out," Jack shouted and charged.

Muller was bigger and heavier than Jack, but the young man's momentum drove him into the hallway where they crashed to the floor. Jack was skinny and undernourished, but the strength that comes from rage overwhelmed Muller, and all he could do was fight to hold Jack's arms, knowing his strength would soon subside. Jack was writhing and fighting to free his arms, but he was weakening. Muller rolled over on top of him and knelt on his biceps pinning him on his back. "Cool it, Jack, I just want to talk to you," Muller said, seeing the rash and a large meth scab on his face.

"Fuck you," Jack yelled, using every ounce of his remaining strength in a futile attempt to push Muller off. Then without warning he blacked out.

"You've killed him," Jasmine screamed. "Get off him, get off him."

"He's all right. He's just blacked out from overexertion and lack of food," Muller said. "See the rashes and scab on his face? They're proof of meth addiction. Sam, get Anneka's number from Jack's cell phone while you can and send it to me with the photos."

"Okay," Sam said, skimming through Jack's contacts.

"Jasmine, Jack needs professional help, and we need to get him checked into a drug rehabilitation clinic tonight."

"Tonight?" Jasmine gasped.

"I have contacts at an excellent private clinic and can have him admitted with one call. Just give me the nod."

"I-I-don't know. I'd like to talk to him first."

Muller slowly shook his head. "You don't get it, do you? He's sick. He's an addict, and he may be for the rest of his life. I can guarantee this clinic will get him clean again, but I can't guarantee he'll stay that way. No one can. There's no time to talk."

"He's right, Mom," Sam said.

As Jack started to stir, Jasmine said, "How are you going to get him admitted. He's eighteen, he's an adult. I can't sign his admission papers."

"You can if he's seventeen," Muller said.

"You want me to lie?"

"A white lie. I'll call an ambulance. Sam, get your brother a glass of water."

"He won't stay. I know he won't. He'll check himself out in the morning." Jasmine sobbed. "I know he will."

"I can promise you he won't be discharged for at least five days and hopefully by then he'll realize it's for his own good."

"He won't," Jasmine said. "He's changed. He won't listen to the doctors. He won't listen to me. He won't listen to anyone."

The ambulance arrived promptly, but not before Jack had regained his belligerence. "I'm not fucking going," he yelled, futilely trying to break Muller's firm grip on his arm.

"What's he on?" One of the ambos asked.

"Ice," Muller said.

"I'll give him a mild sedative, and strap him to a stretcher while we still can," the ambo said. "With luck, it'll stop him from going crazy on the way to the clinic."

"I'm coming with you, Jack," Jasmine said.

"No, you're not. It's not safe," Muller said. "I'll go with him, and you can follow in your car."

Douglas Aspine moved quickly once he received the call from Mick McHugh and was elated when he saw the ambulance in Jasmine's driveway and the frenetic activity on the veranda. He took photos and videoed the activities, and when the ambulance departed, he too followed it.

Chapter 39

THE DRIVE BACK FROM the clinic was tense, and Jasmine wrestled with her conscience over what she had just done. *What type of mother puts her son into a drug rehabilitation clinic?* "He's not going to stay in there," she said. "He's going to bolt the first opportunity he gets."

"You'll be able to talk to him in a few days' time, and maybe you'll be able to convince him that it's for his own good to stay," Muller said.

"He won't listen to anyone. I already told you that."

"What about Uncle Raj, Mom?" Sam said. "Jack really respects him."

"Perhaps, but that was before Jack got sick," Jasmine said. "I'll call him when we get home. It would be wonderful if he could come down, wouldn't it, Sam?"

Muller didn't say anything but knew that along with Jasmine, Raj, had been responsible for framing Aspine, and he wondered whether luring Raj from Singapore was part of Aspine's grand plan. As if she was reading his mind, Jasmine said, "This is why you asked me about Douglas Aspine, isn't it? He's the bastard responsible for getting Jack hooked on drugs, isn't he? Is he in Australia?"

"Yes, all of his old enemies, including you, have suffered since his escape from Changi. I suspect he's here but can't say for sure. He could well be pulling the strings from overseas, but for what it's worth, I think he's back."

"But why would he want to hurt Jack?"

"Is there anything more painful than watching a loved one suffer?" Muller sighed. "He knows he can hurt you far more through your children than he can by directly attacking you."

"Bastard!"

"If Raj comes down, you should tell him to be on his guard, because if I'm right, Aspine will be expecting him and who knows what he might have planned."

"Oh, I didn't think of that. Maybe it would be better if I didn't ask him."

"Don't be silly, Mom." Sam interrupted. "Uncle Raj knows how to look after himself, and think of how good he'll be for Jack."

Douglas Aspine poured himself a Jack Daniels, threw his legs up on the sofa and grinned. He had followed the ambulance to the drug rehabilitation clinic and watched Jack get admitted from the safety of the street. Photos of Jack and a video of him getting strapped to a stretcher were already doing the rounds on YouTube. Life was great. *If I'm lucky, the little prick will be permanently addicted, and his bitch of a mother will suffer for the rest of her life knowing that her frame-up was the cause.* There was only one to go; the bitch's brother, Singapore billionaire, Raj George.

Chin answered his phone on the second ring with a terse hello.

"Chin, it's me."

"Who is this?"

"It's your old flat-mate from Australia. Surely you haven't forgotten me?"

"I'm not sure I know who you are. I don't recognize your voice."

"That's testimony to Sonchai's skills. He's a very fine craftsman."

There was a long pause. "Chin, are you still there?"

"Sure, I was just thinking. Tell me, when we shared that flat, what did I call you?"

"Old man," Aspine replied. "I didn't like it then, and I don't like it now."

"And where did our mutual friend travel to?"

"Brazil."

"Ah, it is you. I presume you're phoning because it's time to activate our contract?"

"Yes. Are you in Singapore?"

"No, I'm not stupid." Chin laughed. "I'll never set foot in there again, but that doesn't mean I'm not in control."

"I'm transferring the fee tonight. Is it the same account as last time?"

"Yes."

"You'll have your money in the morning. Do you envisage any problems?"

"There will be no problems. Our target has many servants, and two of them are on my payroll."

Chapter 40

BILL MULLER STARED AT the photos of Anneka he'd down-loaded to his laptop, and it was easy to see why Jack Bartlett had been seduced by her. She was a stunning young woman. When he had called her number, he got the message that he'd expected, *this number is no longer in service.* He was sure she had used a prepaid cell phone, and his contacts on the force had been quick to confirm this. At his request, they had also provided him with an alphabetical list of escort agencies that Jack McHugh controlled in Australia. There were more than twenty. Muller marveled at the size of McHugh's empire. He was a one finger typist, and he slowly Googled his way down the list on his desktop checking the pictures of the girls with Anneka's. There were only three agencies left when he reached T, and he was starting to think that he might be wrong when he hit pay dirt. The girls at The Executive Suite were young, beautiful and pricey and the most expensive item on the flesh menu was Candy, aka Anneka Nordstrom.

The events of the night and admitting poor Jack to the drug rehabili-tation clinic had weighed heavily on Jasmine and pushed her to the edge. She was stressed and fearful knowing how the hate in Douglas Aspine must have festered over the years, but never thinking that he'd get out and seek revenge by hurting her kids.

What an evil bastard. I thought he'd be an old man when he got out of Changi, but he's back. Worse, what's he going to do next? Jasmine thought.

It was midnight when Jasmine called Raj but 10 P.M. in Singapore. He had been at his office for fourteen hours when he picked up the line reserved for VIPs. He listened in silence as Jasmine sobbed her way through telling him what had happened with Jack and that the former detective, Bill Muller, thought Douglas Aspine was behind it. Raj didn't tell her that he had feared for her after Aspine had escaped and that he had had a security company watching her. Now he cursed his stupidity.

Why didn't I have the kids watched? Hurting them was just the type of revenge that the slimy, characterless Douglas Aspine would dream up.

"Raj, can you come down? I don't know how long we can keep Jack in the drug rehabilitation clinic. He'll listen to you. Please say *yes*."

"I have a function to attend with the Minister for Trade tomorrow night. It will be seen as an insult, if I try to back out at this late stage. I can be on an early flight on Wednesday morning that will put me in Melbourne in the evening."

There was a long pause. "Jasmine, are you still there?"

"Why are you taking a commercial flight? And why can't you fly out as soon as the function is over? I was hoping that you might be able to leave straight away. It will be three days before you're here, and Jack might have checked out of the clinic by then. I hate putting pressure on you, but I'm worried sick." Jasmine sniffled.

"I wasn't anticipating using the jet in the next week, so I lent it to a colleague who's now in Switzerland. I understand your concern, my little sister, but you must stay strong. If the function finishes early, I'll be on the midnight flight. Try and hold up. It's the best I can do."

"I'll meet you at the airport, Raj. Bill Muller told me that I should warn you to be careful because Douglas Aspine will be anticipating your arrival, and may have something planned."

Raj knew what a snake Aspine was and had little doubt that something nasty lay in store for him in Melbourne. *I wonder whether he'll try to kill me?* he thought. "Thanks, but I'll organize a limo from the airport, and don't worry about me, I can look after myself. Besides, the former detective is only speculating, and he may well be wrong. With luck, I'll see you around midday on Wednesday."

"You're just saying that to reassure me. It's him, all right. I love you, Raj. Please be careful."

Mary Denton had become a recluse. She never left the house not even venturing into the garden for fear that she might run across a neighbor. The guest room in the house was fully self-contained, and she moved into it, leaving Harry to look after himself. He did all the shopping always ensuring he bought enough groceries and fruit and vegetables to keep Mary going as well. The mood in the house was tense, but it was thawing, and one night Mary finally came out of her self-imposed exile to watch the news and a quiz show with Harry. They talked, only small talk and nothing significant but it was breaking the ice. Harry was grateful. The money in the freezer was still gnawing at him, and he was dying to ask her about it but decided to wait for a more opportune time. By the end of the week, they had watched four nights television together, and the atmosphere was decidedly warmer.

"Darling," Harry said, "I have to ask you something. Where did you get the cash, you put in the freezer?"

"What? What are you talking about?" Mary responded defensively. "I don't know anything about any cash."

"There's eight thousand in the freezer. Come out to the kitchen, and I'll show you."

Harry opened the freezer and rummaged around the back before removing a frozen wad of hundred-dollar bills. "Now do you recall putting it there?"

"I've never seen that money before, and I'd never hide anything in the freezer, let alone cash. I'd don't know how it got there." Mary paused. "That is unless you planted it."

"Why would I do that?"

"Because you're determined to have me committed. I'm an embarrassment, so you want to get me out of the way. Go on, admit it, Harry."

"I love you, Mary, and that is the last thing I would want. I didn't hide that cash. Think, what use would I have for it?"

"I can ask you the same question."

Harry looked at his feet not sure whether he should say anything, but if he didn't, he'd never know. "It's the exact balance that would've been owed on the driveway had the contractors finished it. The boss said that you gave him two thousand in an envelope when you signed the order, and when he put it in his pocket, it nearly froze his leg off."

"I never signed any order, and I never gave him two thousand! He's a liar, Harry. A liar. Why don't you believe me?" Mary screamed.

"Are you sure you didn't forget? I didn't put the cash in the freezer, so how did it get there?"

"Someone's trying to hurt us, Harry." Mary sobbed. "Can't you see that?"

"What, and they broke into our house and planted a wad of cash in our freezer? Hardly likely," Harry said.

"Go ahead then. Make the arrangements to have me committed to a nursing home. That's what you've wanted all along," Mary yelled, storming out of the kitchen.

Harry hung his head. *What am I going to do?*

Chapter 41

SQ237 TOUCHED DOWN AT 10:20 A.M., and as expected, Raj George was escorted from his first-class cubicle to Tullamarine's VIP waiting room. It was nothing new, and he had been there many times before albeit for only the few minutes it took to clear customs. What was new was the increase in the number of officials, and the beagle and its handler.

One of the customs officials greeted him warmly. "Welcome to Melbourne, sir. Do you have anything to declare?"

"No, nothing," Raj said, surprised to see the beagle straining against its leash.

"Did you pack your suitcase?"

"Yes," Raj replied, which wasn't true because his valet had packed it, but he just didn't have time to go into lengthy explanations.

"Please open your suitcase, sir."

On countless trips to Australia, Raj had never had to open his suitcase before. "Is there something wrong?"

"Nothing, sir. It's just routine."

As Raj flicked his suitcase open, the beagle nearly tore its handler's arm socket out trying to get to it. *Oh no! No! I know what that dog's going to find.* "I didn't pack my suitcase. My valet did."

"Are you concerned about what the dog might find? If so, it would be better to come clean now and save us all a lot of time.'

"No, no, you don't understand."

Raj's clothes were spread out on the bench in front of him, and the beagle strained to get to a navy-blue pinstripe suit coat. One of the customs officials held it up. It was obviously hand tailored, and the lining seemed to blend seamlessly with the fabric. "We're just going to x-ray your suit coat, sir." The customs official said, handing it to an assistant.

"It's a frame-up," Raj said. "Can't you see that? I'm a billionaire! Why would I want to smuggle anything?"

"Are you confessing, sir? Do you want to tell us what's hidden in the lining?"

"No, no, you fool. I haven't hidden anything."

"That's not true," the assistant said, holding up the suit coat with the stitching in the lining unpicked, to reveal a thin fabric bag. "There's over a hundred grams of heroin in there."

"It was planted," Raj shouted. "Can't you fools see that?"

Two burly plain clothed policemen took Raj by the elbows and escorted him to a waiting car. Surprisingly, the car was surrounded by reporters, photographers and television crews. A tall man was smiling at the back of the press pack.

Despite all charges being dropped, Sir Edwin Philby was in the depths of despair and woke up each day contemplating suicide. The family name had been destroyed, and he would forever be remembered as a pedophile. It was only with great reluctance that he had agreed to see Bill Muller at his office. His secretary had resigned after he had been charged and the thought of interviewing a replacement was just too much for him. "What can I do for you?" He tersely asked Muller.

"I know you were set up, and I know who did it."

"What?"

"Hasn't anyone contacted you? Fiona Jeczik, Harry Denton or Jasmine Bartlett?"

"No, why would they? I hardly know the two women, and Harry hasn't spoken to me since I was dismissed as Mercury's chairman. He can be grumpy, you know."

"You didn't read about what happened to Fiona and Harry's wife?"

"No, I didn't. I haven't read a newspaper or watched the news in months. Why would I, with what they've been saying about me? Now get to the point, man."

"I'm nearly certain that Douglas Aspine set you up, and he's done the same to Fiona, Harry, and Jasmine. Like you, their lives are in tatters."

"So, it was him," Sir Edwin said, the color returning to his face. "I racked my brain trying to think who could hate me that much and be so evil as to do what he did. Of course, it was him. What did he do to the others?"

Muller explained in great detail what he thought Aspine had done.

"What are we going to do?" Sir Edwin asked.

"Jasmine's brother, Raj, is flying in from Singapore. When he arrives, I think we should meet and try to come up with a plan that will help us find Aspine and put him back in prison."

"Have you told Harry about Aspine?"

"No. Like what you said, he's a crusty old bugger who's unlikely to confide in me. He was close to Fiona Jeczik though, and I've asked her to talk to him."

"What a disgusting piece of work that man is, and to think I was the one who made him CEO of Mercury. You've lifted a huge load off my shoulders, detective. I'll never regain my reputation, but it's a relief to know who set me up. If he's in Australia, I'll make the bastard pay. God, I'll make him pay."

"It's not detect–"

"Set the meeting up, detective," Sir Edwin interrupted. "We need to stop him before he does any more damage. Oh, and you'd better get out to the airport and warn Jasmine's brother to be alert."

Jasmine busied herself tidying up the house while waiting for Raj. Just before midday she flicked the television on to catch the news and was shocked to see her brother shielding his face from photographers and television cameras.

"Billionaire Singaporean businessman, Mr. Raj George, has been detained by police after a large quantity of heroin was found in his luggage," a somber newsreader intoned. "Mr. George has been taken to police headquarters in St Kilda Road where he is helping police with their inquiries." Jasmine gasped, unable to think. *Why hasn't he called me?* She knew Raj's Melbourne lawyer and immediately called him, only to be told by his PA that he was aware of the situation and was en route to police headquarters. Jasmine ran from the house, climbed into her car and headed toward St Kilda Road.

The detectives transporting Raj to headquarters had obviously been briefed about how important he was and were quite respectful. However, when he asked if he could use his phone, he was told that he had two calls and to make the most of them. The first was to his Melbourne lawyer and the second to Singapore's deputy prime minister where much to the chagrin of the police, he spoke in Malay.

Harry Denton hadn't liked leaving Mary, not even for an hour, but he had needed a haircut desperately. On his return, he was surprised and then concerned when he opened the garage door, and her car was gone. He hurried into the house yelling, "Mary! Mary, are you there?" There was no answer, and then Harry noticed an envelope on the kitchen table that he tore open.

Dear Harry,

I cannot live like this any longer, with you looking at me like a hawk and wanting to have me committed.

We no longer talk. You just ask me questions and then wait for me to make mistakes with my answers that will confirm your thoughts that I'm losing it. I'm not! I did not lose my car, I did not order that book, I did not order a new driveway, I did not steal that cashmere top, and I have no idea where that cash in the freezer came from. Someone must really hate me to have gone to so much trouble to make it look like I am losing my marbles. It distresses me to know that you no longer trust me, preferring instead to think that I am demented. I cannot tell you how much this loss of trust has hurt me.

Harry, I hate doing this, but I can no longer live with you. I have rented a small apartment, and you will no longer have to worry yourself about placing me in a nursing home. I've left my cell phone in your study — please don't try to contact me.

Good luck,

Mary

Harry's face was ghostly white as he slumped into a kitchen chair with his head in his hands and wept uncontrollably.

Chapter 42

THE POLICE HAD PAID Raj a great deal of respect, and after he'd been fingerprinted and had mug shots taken, he was shown to an interrogation room fitted out with audiovisual equipment. "Would you like something to drink?" one of the detectives asked.

"Thank you for your kindness, no. My lawyer will be here soon, and in the meantime, I do not intend to answer any of your questions."

"If you were to waive your right to a lawyer, we might be able to help you," the detective said.

"You should be glad that I'm going to forget you said that, detective," Raj said scornfully. "Perhaps I did not make myself clear. I will not answer any questions until my lawyer is here."

"Spoken like a guilty man." The detective sneered.

Thirty minutes later, with his lawyer sitting next to him, Raj denied that he had knowingly brought any heroin into the country. He insisted what had been found, had been planted. The police were dogged but circumspect. It was rare for drug dealers to be represented by a powerful law firm like Hollinghills. They knew that any slip-ups would find their way back to their superiors and result in disciplinary action. After the interrogation was over, the lawyer sought and was granted permission for a distressed Jasmine to spend ten minutes with her brother.

"Raj." She sobbed, throwing her arms around him. "I'm sorry."

"Why? It is not your fault, my little sister."

"How-how did the drugs get in your luggage?"

"They were planted in one of my suit coats. It was most certainly one of my servants."

"But Chan Chun Hee has been your valet for more than ten years, and he's so loyal. Surely he wouldn't have done such a thing?"

"The gangs in Singapore are vicious and persuasive. What if they

156

threatened him and said that they were going to kill his wife or children if he didn't do what they wanted?"

"That is terrible. How are you going to clear your name?"

"My people in Singapore will track down the culprits. I'll soon know who planted the heroin."

"How are you going to get out?"

"Don't worry. My lawyers are applying for bail as we speak so expect to see me for dinner tonight." Raj smiled.

"God, if only I hadn't asked you to come down, you wouldn't be in this mess. It's all my fault."

"No, it's not. It's the work of an evil, evil man."

"I'm expecting Jack to check out of the drug rehabilitation clinic anytime now," Jasmine said, her face drawn and her brow furrowed in a way that Raj had never seen before. "I'm sorry. You have more than enough of your own troubles now."

"Don't worry about Jack. He won't be checking out until he's completely clean. I hope he isn't, but you do realize that he may be addicted for life."

"How do you know that?"

"Hollinghills are very influential, and I've instructed them to ensure that Jack is not released. If there's a problem, I'll buy the clinic, so you have nothing to worry about. You should also know that I've organized around the clock security for you and the boys."

"You're so calm. How can you be so unflustered at a time like this?"

Before he could answer one of the policemen said, "That's time."

"I'll see you tonight," Raj said as he was led away to the cells.

Aspine spread the morning newspapers across his dining table and gloated. The *Herald-Sun* had gone with the headline *Drug Mr. Big Apprehended* and *The Age, Beagled,* with a photo of the dog and a photo of Raj George below it. His lawyers, Hollinghills, one of the most powerful and influential law firms in the land, had made an urgent application for bail, but the judge had refused and instead remanded Raj in custody until Monday.

I wonder how you're going to like five nights in the cells, you bastard.

And what are you going to tell the court? 'I framed this guy 10 years ago, and now he's framed me as payback.'

Aspine flopped on the couch and flicked the television on. There was a stern looking woman being interviewed on one of the morning shows. "We have to send a message to these drug dealers," she thundered. "God knows how many young lives a hundred grams of heroin would've ruined. It's time we got tough and adopted the sentencing procedures of our Asian neighbors. If this was Singapore, this piece of vermin would be looking at the gallows." Aspine rolled over on his back and immersed himself in the warm glow coursing through him.

There's not a drug in the world that could put me on a greater high.

Fiona Jeczik read the same newspapers which confirmed what she already knew — it was Douglas Aspine who had brought her, Raj, and the others down. Two questions played on her mind. Was he in Australia and had his quest for revenge been satisfied? She was almost certain he was back and reveling in the havoc he was wreaking. If that was so, and he could be found, he could be back in Singapore and in Changi in no time at all. She doubted his desire for vengeance had been satisfied, and her biggest fears were for Jasmine. His hate for her must know no bounds, and Fiona thought murder was not beyond him. There was one man who could stop him and put him back in Changi where he deserved to be. She punched Bill Muller's number into her cell phone and waited for the gravelly voice to answer.

"Bill, it's Fiona. We have to stop this bastard. I'm really scared for Jasmine."

"Don't worry about her. Raj has security guards looking after her twenty-four hours a day."

"How do you know? How could he have organized that from a cell?"

"I went out to the airport yesterday to warn him to be careful, only to see him being carted off to police headquarters. I met his lawyer and Jasmine there. The lawyer told her that Raj had instructed him to make sure that she and kids were protected around the clock. The security firm they're using is top notch, and Aspine won't get close to any of them."

"That's a relief, Bill. Okay, how do we find him and make sure he's incarcerated again?"

"Fiona, we don't even know he's here. He could be sunning himself on a beach in Hawaii, orchestrating everything from there."

"You don't believe that. He's here, watching and relishing the pain he's inflicting."

"Yeah, you're probably right, but that doesn't make the job of finding him any easier. I guess he's had extensive plastic surgery. If I'm right, how do we go about identifying him, let alone finding him?"

"You're the detective," Fiona said with a weak laugh. "Work it out, and Bill, work it out in a hurry."

"We need to have a meeting. Maybe someone has seen something or perhaps even seen him, but paid no attention to it. Any clue would help. Have you spoken to Harry Denton yet?"

"I was meant to see him yesterday for coffee, but he canceled. Mary left him, and he was too distraught to talk. I'm seeing him this afternoon."

"Did you tell him about Aspine?"

"No, he was crying, and it didn't seem appropriate."

"He must know."

"I doubt it. I get the feeling that he's not reading newspapers or watching television these days."

"Poor bugger. Aspine really done him over."

"He's done us all over, Bill."

Chapter 43

ASPINE ENTERED THE CROWDED bar of the Birmingham and saw Mick McHugh, cold beer in hand, surrounded by a small group of acolytes hanging on his every word. Seeing Aspine, he shouted, "Over here," and then looking at the men around him. "Okay, you lot can fuck off. I've got some business to attend to."

"Hello, Mick." Aspine grinned, extending his hand.

"I don't think I've seen a happier man this year. Chin really delivered for you, and then you got lucky when the judge knocked back that prick's bail application. You know he'll make bail on Monday, don't you?"

"How can you be so sure?"

"Because they'll either find the prick who planted the shit or they'll get someone to say he did."

"Get someone to say he did?"

"Yeah, imagine some poor bastard up in Singapore with half a dozen kids being offered a million to say he planted the heroin in the asshole's suit coat, with a guarantee that he won't do any more than ten years. Do ya think he's gonna say no? Do you think that if he says he wants two mil that the prick's going to haggle? Christ, he's a billionaire. A few mil is chicken shit to him."

"Okay, let's say he makes bail. Can he go back to Singapore?"

"Nah, a condition of bail will almost certainly be the surrender of his passport. If the Director of Public Prosecutions doesn't drop the ball, he'll be here until his trial."

"Drop the ball?"

"Yeah, that smartass mob of lawyers he's using will be going all out to prove that there's no case to answer and that he shouldn't even be charged."

"Fuck, I don't want that."

"Why? He's almost certainly going to get off when it gets to trial."

"I know, but the longer he's here, the more chance there is for his enemies to undermine and work against him in Singapore. They'll already be shafting him."

"Enemies? What enemies?"

Aspine laughed. "For someone who knows so much, Mick, you can be awfully naïve. You don't get to be a billionaire without burning a lot of people along the way. They'll be coming out of the woodwork in Asia, doing everything they can to hurt him. The longer he's stuck down here, the better."

Mick McHugh didn't take kindly to being called naïve. "Ya just got fucking lucky, Einstein. The media's all over it, and it's an election year. The government's not gonna let him walk without a trial. Are ya going to hang around for it?"

"No, Raj George will never attain the status and power that he once had, and we've ruined the lives of the others. I'll stay for another few weeks, and that'll be it. Job completed. If I'm really lucky that bitch's son will be addicted for life."

"Do ya want me to fix ya up with a genuine Australian passport before ya go?"

"I think I'm okay in that area." Aspine grinned. "Besides, I'm not sure how genuine it would be or whether I could afford it."

"Oh, it's genuine. I buy the passports and driving licenses off the bums sleeping in parks and under bridges. They'll never use them again. I pay a grand for a passport and five hundred for a license. I gotta tell ya, identity theft is the fastest growing area of my business," McHugh said, snapping his fingers at the barman for another beer. "If they don't have a passport I get one of my lawyers to accompany them to the Passports Office and help fill out the application form. I pay the bums' fees and flip them a grand."

"Yeah, but what happens when they die?" Aspine asked. "The office of Births, Deaths and Marriages notifies immigration and the police department. The poor bastard who's been using the dead guy's identity is screwed."

McHugh laughed. "That's right, but what if they die without being identified? Half the bums have no form of identification when they cark it, or they've been hiding out and using false names. No one can identify them, and they remain as John Does for eternity. Births Deaths and Marriages can't notify immigration or the police."

"Jesus, the buyer has just bought himself an identity for life. How many sets of documents for John Does do you have?"

"At the last count, around six hundred. I'm sure I can fit ya to a set of documents, and all ya have to do is adopt the stiff's name and perfect his signature. I told ya they were genuine."

"How much?"

"Fifty thousand and I'll need a photo," McHugh said, pulling out his iPhone.

"Yeah, fix me up with a set of documents. I'll do the transfer tonight."

I'm getting ripped off, but a genuine Australian passport is worth that to me. I'll never have to worry about customs and immigration again.

"That's a wise decision, and as a gesture of goodwill, I've got a little present for ya."

"Mick, I've got no more money. I've paid you more than a mil, and whatever you've got planned, I can't afford it."

"I said it was a present." McHugh scowled. "If ya gonna be like that ya can fuck off."

"Okay, okay, I'm sorry," Aspine said.

"So ya bloody should be. I thought you might like to spend a night with Candy on me, but if ya'd rather be a smartass, I'll just forget it."

"I said I was sorry, and that's very generous of you, Mick."

"Too bloody right it is," McHugh said, sliding a card for *The Executive Suite* across the table. "Don't forget she's a major asset, so make sure there's no rough stuff. I'd hate to have to break yer legs.

Chapter 44

IT WAS A HOT SUMMER'S day, and Fiona Jeczik sat under a large umbrella out the front of a popular High Street Road coffee shop. Harry Denton had been reluctant to meet with her, but couldn't refuse when she chose a location so close to his home. An old hunched-over man shuffled past the shops, and it was only when he was a few meters away that she saw his distinctive blue eyes.

"Harry," she said, standing and pulling a chair out for him. "Let's get you out of the sun or would you rather go inside?"

"Hello, Fiona," he said, kissing her on the cheek. "I'm fine out here, and I can use the fresh air. If you can call it fresh, that is. Sorry, I can't stay long. I'm hoping Mary will call and I have to get home. You said you had something urgent to discuss with me."

"Have you been reading the newspapers or watching the news on television?"

"That's a strange question. No, I stopped reading and watching the rubbish that passes for news after the media savaged Mary."

"You'd better order a black coffee, Harry, because I'm going tell you a few things about our friend, Douglas Aspine, which might come as a bit of a shock," Fiona said, beckoning to a waiter.

"What about him?"

In the next ten minutes, Fiona related all of the strange events that had occurred in the past few months and Bill Muller's involvement.

Harry didn't say a word, but his mouth was agape. He then told Fiona of the events that had befallen Mary and how she had left him. "But how did the cash get in our freezer? Someone would've had to have broken into our home."

"Bill Muller said that his sources told him that Mick McHugh is somehow involved, and if that's right, your house might well have been broken into. To me it smells of Aspine," Fiona said.

"Mary was telling the truth. Her memory wasn't failing her. God, what have I done?" Harry moaned. "I should've believed her."

"Don't beat up on yourself. Your reaction was normal. It was a cunning scheme."

"Yes, but if I'd trusted her, she'd still be with me."

"Once she knows what happened, she'll come back, Harry. It'll be just like it was before Aspine implemented his rotten schemes."

"She might come back, but it'll never be the same," Harry said, hanging his head. "Do you know where Aspine is?"

"No, he could be orchestrating this whole thing from a safe haven overseas."

Harry paused. "No way. I know him and how he thinks. He's here, and he's watching the pain unfold in front of him. That's his style. Sorry, I have to fly," he said, giving her a peck on the forehead. "I don't want to miss Mary, if she calls. Thanks, Fiona. It's a relief to know what really happened and that Mary's okay. If only I'd believed her."

Fiona watched as Harry walked away and thought she noticed a little bounce in his step.

Aspine was euphoric after his meeting with Mick McHugh and called The Executive Suite on the drive back to his apartment. The receptionist knew who he was the minute he said his name. "Mr. Adderley, we've been expecting your call," she said. "When would you like to see Candy?"

"Tonight, at eight o'clock works for me."

"Hold on. I'll just check her availability." A few seconds later she said, "Yes, that's fine, Candy's looking forward to meeting you."

"My address is—"

"We know where you reside, Mr. Adderley."

I never told Mick where I lived. He must have had me followed. I won't be here for much longer, but I need to be careful with him.

Bill Muller was anxious to set up a group meeting, but Jasmine wouldn't hear of it until Raj was released and could also be there. Muller didn't say anything but was far from convinced the court would grant Raj's bail application. He was more concerned about Aspine becoming violent and looking to harm or kill Jasmine or her children. She told him not to worry, and that Raj had security guards looking after them. "Arrange your meeting for Monday night at my home," she said. "Raj will be free by then."

"Sure," he replied, no less concerned. Aspine by the actions he'd taken against Jack and Raj had not tried to hide his involvement. He was not the type of man to anonymously seek revenge; he had to let them know it was him. If Muller was correct, Aspine would now move to the fear phase of his vengeance, or perhaps something deadlier. He was not convinced that the security guards would be smart enough to protect Jasmine and her family. In all his years as a policeman, he'd never met anyone as Machiavellian as Douglas Aspine.

Chapter 45

CANDY ARRIVED AT ASPINE'S apartment right on time, carrying a small overnight bag. She was wearing a sleeveless, light blue cotton dress with matching sandals. Aspine thought that the photos he had seen didn't do her justice. The blueness of her unblinking eyes was haunting, and he found it hard to hold her gaze. "Hi, Charles. I'm Candy," she said, holding out her hand before quickly withdrawing it.

"What's wrong?" Aspine asked.

"We're in the middle of a heat wave, and you're getting around in gloves. What's your story?"

"It's nothing. I had my hands and lower arms mangled in an accident, and I always wear gloves when I go out. I forgot to take them off when I got back," he said, peeling one glove off.

She took his hand and turned it over. "It's not all that bad," she said. "It's only the palms and fingers that are severely scarred. It must have been terribly painful."

"Yeah, yeah," he said. "Can I get you something to drink?"

She laughed. "You don't want to talk about it. That's fine. Do you have sparkling mineral water?"

"Sure," he shouted from the kitchen. "How do you know Mick McHugh?"

"I don't really. I've met him a few times, and I know he owns the agency, but I really have nothing to do with him."

"I'm confused. Who's your boss then?"

"A supervisor runs the agency, and he's my boss."

"Yeah, but if you had a falling out with your supervisor you'd complain to Mick."

"No, there's a manager in charge of the escort agencies. He visits a few times a month. If I had a gripe, I'd let him know, but I've never had one."

"Far out," Aspine said, flopping on the sofa. "Mick runs the agencies just like you'd run a corporation. You might be interested to know that he describes you as one of his major assets."

"I know. His manager's told me that before." She smiled.

"Mick organized for you to be here. Has he ever done that before?"

"You've got a lot of questions. I learned long ago that you stay healthy in this business by keeping your mouth shut. So long as I earn what I'd normally earn, I just do what I'm told. If I'm getting paid to service a John, then I service him."

"I'm not a John." Aspine scowled and then forced a smile. "Tell me has Mick ever paid you to service anyone before?"

"No," Candy lied, "You're the first."

"I bet." Aspine smirked. "Okay, that's enough foreplay. Let's go in the bedroom."

He kicked off his shirt and pants and jumped on the bed. "I want to watch you undress. Do it slowly."

"Fine," Candy said.

Aspine enjoyed what he was seeing. She had a lithe, tanned body, teardrop breasts, and long, toned legs. When she was down to her G-string, he said, "Come over here." He wasn't quite ready and placed her hand on his semi-aroused penis. A few minutes later he mounted and thrust himself deep inside of her. The feel of his scarred hands on her body sent tremors down her spine. As he rolled off and turned his back to her, she noticed the finely stitched scars behind his ears and, these together with the scar she had felt on his stomach told her that he'd had extensive plastic surgery. He swung around abruptly to face her. "What are you looking at?"

"I was admiring your surgeon's skills."

"What the fuck are you talking about?" he snarled.

"I can see the stitches behind your ears, and I felt the scar on your stomach. Don't get touchy. No one's ever going to pick that you've had a facelift. Who's your surgeon? He did a great job."

Fuck, she's a smart bitch, and there's no point denying it. "Why do you want to know?"

"I'm thinking about getting a boob job," she lied. "I've been on the lookout for a good surgeon and your guy looks the goods."

Aspine cupped one of her breasts in his hand, not noticing the look of revulsion that passed across her face. "You don't need a boob job, honey. Well not yet anyway, and when you do, my surgeon's in Bangkok, and he's far too expensive for you."

"I don't think so."

"You'd be shocked at how pricey he is. He has a special group of clients. Here," he said, putting her hand on one of his love handles. "I'm seeing him in the next few weeks to get rid of these."

"They're not that bad," she said. "You're very vain."

"They're ugly. I bet your younger clients don't have them."

"I don't have young clients. How could they afford me?"

"What about a boyfriend?"

"You can't have boyfriends in a job like this. There'll be time for them in few years' time after I've set myself up and finished working."

You're a good liar. You're not going to breathe a word about Jack Bartlett, are you? "So, when was the last time you were with a young guy?"

"Jeez, you ask a lot of questions. So long ago, I can't remember." Candy laughed. "I'm going to the bathroom."

He watched her stroll out of the bedroom, totally starkers, seemingly without a care in the world. *If you weren't one of Mick McHugh's major assets, I'd soon loosen your tongue with a few well-timed backhanders.* She certainly didn't lack confidence and why would she with her looks and body? Her tan contrasted against the tiny white part that her bikini covered and he felt a slight stirring. He hadn't thought about firing two shots since his escape. Perhaps now was the time. When she returned, she stood in the doorway. "Do you want to watch some telly?"

"Fuck the television. I like your landing strip." He grinned. "Why don't you bring it over here?"

He groped her breasts and put one hand between her legs but the stirring he'd felt had vanished. Angry, he seized her hand and placed it around his limp dick, and when that failed, he grabbed her behind the neck forcing her head down. "No, no, not without a condom," she gasped, pulling away.

"I'm clean. I don't have syphilis or AIDS. And how are we going to bloody well get a condom on?"

"Hang on," she said, standing up and opening her overnight bag. "I'll just get a glass of water." When she returned, she handed him the glass with a little blue tablet. "This will solve your little problem."

"Viagra! Fucking Viagra. I don't need that shit." Aspine scowled, throwing the tablet away. "We're done. You can show yourself out."

Candy dressed quickly. "Goodbye," she said.

As she reached the front door, Aspine yelled, "I bet you made damn sure that young Jack never had any trouble getting it up more than once."

She paused before pulling the door open. *So that's why the weirdo asked so many questions about young guys. He was the client, and that's why Mick made him a gift of me. I wonder what Jack did to the asshole?*

Chapter 46

"CONGRATULATIONS RAJ," MULLER SAID. "I have to say I thought you might still be in the cells."

"Bail was never in doubt. If that fool of a judge hadn't been grandstanding last week, I wouldn't have even spent one night in the cells. I had to surrender my passport, but I expect to get it back within a few weeks."

"When do you go to trial?"

"In six months, but the charges will be dropped long before then. I'll never go to trial. My lawyers will prove beyond any doubt that I was framed."

"I don't believe you've met Sir Edwin Philby, Raj," Jasmine said. "And this is Fiona Jeczik and Harry Denton."

"I'd like to say it's a pleasure, but under the circumstances, I cannot. I do, of course, know of your backgrounds, and Jasmine has told me what Aspine has done to each of you. He is pure evil. I don't know what else he has planned, but we must stop him."

"Let's go into the dining room. Mr. Muller, you know more than anyone else. You sit at the head of the table," Jasmine said.

"Please, it's Bill." Muller sighed, knowing it would make no difference. "Let's get started. Firstly, does everyone agree that Douglas Aspine is behind the events that have befallen you?"

There were murmured assents from around the table.

"Do you think he's here or is he orchestrating everything from overseas?" Muller asked.

"He's here, and he's very close by," Harry said.

"I agree," Fiona said. "It wouldn't surprise me if he took those pics and video of Jack that are on the net."

"Tha-that means he was out the front and followed us to the

clinic," Jasmine gasped. "He was here watching Jack get loaded in the ambulance."

"Settle down, my sister. I promise you he'll not get that close again. What do you think, Bill?"

"I'm not so sure he's here, but if he is, I'm sure that he no longer looks anything like he once did. The man who I believe is helping him, Mick McHugh, is more than capable of engineering these setups."

"This is the first I've heard of this McHugh. Why can't we approach him, and if he won't cooperate, put the police on him?" Raj asked.

Before Muller could reply, Fiona said, "Mick McHugh is Australia's John Gotti. Our most feared criminal. He has vast resources including a small army of thugs who'd kill you as soon as look at you. Even the police are wary of him."

"That's right," Muller agreed. "He won't tell us anything, and the police won't approach him without solid evidence. Raj, what did your people find out in Singapore?"

"Four of my servants have disappeared including my valet who's been with me for over ten years. I trust him implicitly. I think that two of my servants, gardeners, were thugs and members of one of the gangs. I suspect they threatened to harm to my valet's family unless he helped them plant the drugs. He has vanished, and I fear he may be dead."

"If Douglas Aspine walked into this room right now, I'd kill him," Harry said.

Fiona rested her hand on his. "Have you heard from Mary?"

"Not a word. She's disappeared," Harry said, fighting back the tears.

"Harry, I'll find her," Muller said. "After we've finished, let me have her credit card and bank account details along with her vehicle registration. I'll find her within forty-eight hours. Don't worry."

"Can we get back to finding Aspine if he's here?" Raj asked. "Does anyone have any suggestions where we might start?"

"Hold on," Muller said. "I want you all to think whether you've seen anyone loitering or out of place. Someone who's quite tall. Someone who engaged you in conversation. Someone you might have felt uneasy about?"

There were only blank faces and shaking heads.

"That makes me think he's orchestrating everything from overseas. That would be the smart thing to do," Muller said.

"Bill, he's here," Sir Edwin said. "Of that I am certain."

"If he's here and we can find him, we can put him back in Changi. Have we got anything? Something that resembles a lead," Raj said.

"Only the girl who seduced Jack. She works in one of McHugh's escort agencies," Muller replied.

"Anneka's a prostitute," Jasmine gasped.

"Sorry, I didn't want to have to tell you about her, Jasmine. Oh, and the name she goes by at the agency is Candy."

"It's not much of a lead," Raj said. "All it does is take us to McHugh, and we know he's not going to say anything. Is it even worth questioning her?"

"My bloody oath, it is. When I was in the force, and we were getting nowhere with an investigation, we used to start shaking trees, and you'd be amazed at some of the stuff that fell out. I want to shake Candy's tree."

"You do that, Bill," Raj said. "I'll put some more pressure on my people in Singapore to see if they can come up with something. Remember, be vigilant. I don't think he's finished yet. I'd give a million dollars to know what he looks like. As soon as anyone knows anything, we'll have another meeting. And Bill, don't think that we don't appreciate what you are doing. He hasn't hurt you, so you have no reason to be involved. You are a good man. I intend to reward you generously for your time, and if you need help, perhaps the assistance of a private detective or the need to pay a bribe, please don't hesitate. I will cover all of your expenses. If he's here, and we can catch him, the Australian Government will extradite him."

After the others had left, Jasmine asked, "Are you all right, Raj. You look tired and worried."

"I'm fine, but I have some powerful enemies in Singapore who are trying to undermine me. Some are saying that I made my money as a drug runner. I need to get back for a few days."

"I'm sorry. I've caused you so much trouble."

"It wasn't you. So long as I have more friends than enemies, everything will be all right. I need to get back home to make sure that my friends don't switch sides."

"Maybe we were wrong to frame him," Jasmine said.

"Don't ever think that. He is pure evil. Had the authorities done their job properly we would never have had to do what we did. He is scum, Jasmine, and don't ever forget he drove your beloved Kerry to suicide."

Chapter 47

THE EXECUTIVE SUITE WAS located in a two-story Edwardian terrace on the outskirts of the city in upmarket East Melbourne. Bill Muller had called on the pretext of being a punter and been told that Candy would be on the premises until 8 P.M. The receptionist had also let him know that Candy was very expensive and that perhaps one of the other girls would be more to his liking. He'd said he would think about it and get back to her. It was 7:30 P.M., and he was parked in the street with a clear view of the building and the laneway to a small car park at the rear. He hadn't seen any of the punters use the car park, instead preferring the two-hour meters in the street. After waiting forty minutes, Muller watched as a silver CLK Mercedes convertible barreled down the laneway and onto the street. He hit the accelerator and followed it along Victoria Street until it turned abruptly into the Victoria Gardens Shopping Centre. As he drove into the car park, he saw Candy get out of the Merc and walk briskly toward the shops. She hadn't bothered to put the roof up so he knew he wouldn't have long to wait.

Ten minutes later she returned carrying two plastic bags. As she climbed in behind the steering wheel, Muller moved. He was wearing a gray suit, his collar was unbuttoned, and the knot in his tie was halfway down his shirt. His suit coat was undone, and as he stood above Candy, his shoulder holster was clearly visible, though she couldn't know there was no gun in it.

"Candy," he said, flashing his wallet. "I'm Bill Muller. How's the ice business?"

"Bloody coppers," She moaned. "I don't know what you're talking about."

"Really? I have a statement from Jack Bartlett stating that Anneka Nordstrom regularly provided him with ice over a three-month period. You wouldn't happen to know Anneka would you?" Muller grinned.

"Smartass," she said. "I want to talk to my lawyer."

"I don't think you do. I think you want to talk to Mick but unfortunately you can't because he's been otherwise detained," Muller lied. "Besides, you haven't been charged with anything, so you don't need a lawyer. I'm not interested in you, but I am interested in the low-life who put you up to it."

"Put me up to what?"

"Don't get funny with me. You got the kid started on ice, and then you got him hooked. Now he's in a drug rehabilitation clinic, he may never get back to his studies, and you could've ruined his life. His mom's sick with stress and his younger brother's a complete mess. You're not a very nice person, are you? If it was up to me, I'd make sure you were charged with trafficking and did at least a year behind bars, but those who I report to are prepared to let you go if you cooperate and come clean."

"I want to go off the record."

"I can live with that."

"I liked Jack, and I hated what happened to him, but you have to understand, once I was told what to do, I had no choice."

"Yeah, I know, Mick can be very persuasive."

"It wasn't him, and even if it was, I wouldn't tell you. I want to live."

"If it wasn't him, it was one of his lieutenants, wasn't it?"

"I-I can't say."

"Christ, why did you want to go off the record? You've told me nothing. Do you have any idea who the client is?"

"Not the slightest."

Muller stared at her. She'd paused for just a second before answering, just long enough to tell him that she was lying. "Candy, I want to help you, but you've gotta help me. You know who he is."

"No. No, I don't. Well, not for certain."

"Tell me about him. I'll check him out. No one will ever know you told me."

"I need to think about it. Give me your phone number. I'll call you in the morning."

Muller handed her one of his old cards with all the phone numbers except his cell phone crossed out. "The office numbers have changed. I'm getting new cards printed," he lied. "Don't talk to anyone about our conversation because if we end up without someone else to charge, you'll be going to jail for as long as we can put you there." *Christ, if I get caught using that card, it'll be me heading off to jail.*

"If I decide to help you, I don't want to go to a police station, I won't make a statement, and I won't be a witness in any court proceedings. And if we meet, you'll be the only cop there. Do you understand?"

"Sorry, I'm going to have a sketch artist with me. Don't worry. We'll meet at my home. When I know you're coming, I'll leave my garage door open, and you can drive straight in. No one will ever know we met."

"Don't count your chickens. I may decide that I can't help you."

"You mean *won't,* and if you're silly enough not to help, I promise you, you're going to jail, and you'll learn a few things in a women's prison that even in your profession you've never experienced before," Muller said, his demeanor deadly serious. *And that bullshit will add two years to my sentence* he thought.

"I got the message before," Candy snapped, turning on the ignition. "I'll sleep on it."

Mick McHugh was in his usual place when Aspine entered the bar of the Birmingham but surprisingly, was by himself. He looked up and grinned. "G'day, Mr. Schmitt."

"What are you on about, Mick?"

"That's your new name; Osker Schmitt," Mick said, pushing a folder over to Aspine, marked *Osker Elias Schmitt.*

"Osker fucking Schmitt. Fuck, how'd you come up with that?"

"Look at passport and driver's license."

The likeness was incredible, and if Aspine had parted his hair on the other side, it was an almost perfect match. The driving license was eight years old, so the photo was of a younger man, but the similarity was uncanny. There was a birth certificate, and a brief history of Osker's life. He'd been born forty-six years ago in Sydney to German immigrant parents. "Have the photos been doctored?"

"Nope, they're the originals. Ya got lucky with the match, and better still, Osker was an only child with no relatives in Australia. I shoulda charged ya a hundred thousand. You're set up for the rest of ya life."

"How'd you make the match?"

"My people stuck your photo in the computer and then matched it against the six hundred already stored. Then up came Osker."

Aspine was no longer surprised by the expertise McHugh seemed to have at his fingertips. "You didn't tamper with the passport and license in any way?"

"Didn't touch 'em. All you have to do is master Osker's signature."

"Pity it's such shit of a name. I don't know that I like being the son of Krauts."

"Jeez, Osker, I don't think it's much of a sacrifice. Who's to say it won't grow on ya."

"Yeah, you're right, Mick." Aspine laughed, while still staring at the passport. "The match is freakish."

"When are ya gonna start using your new name?"

"I'm not sure. I'll have to think about it." *This afternoon, but you don't need to know. I've still got time to open a bank account and get a debit card. And I'll definitely be flying out as Osker. You don't know it, but this will be the last time I'll see you, Mick.*

"Ya got time for lunch?"

"Sure, Mick. I'm feeling a bit peckish."

"Good. Ya can tell me how Candy performed."

"Yeah."

Chapter 48

ASPINE HAD ONLY REMAINED in Melbourne to see the outcome of Raj George's preliminary hearing and application for bail. He'd expected Raj to be bailed but nonetheless was still disappointed. Now it was time to get out and makes plans for a life in Paraguay or Brazil. He wasn't totally happy with the havoc he had wreaked. His enemies had gotten off lightly, but he had the option of returning as Osker Schmitt and undertaking something far more serious. The thought of killing Jasmine Bartlett and her smartass brother brought him enormous satisfaction, and having criminal contacts in two continents gave him the means.

He closed the bank account in the name of Charles Adderley by withdrawing nearly thirty thousand in cash. Because of the size of the cash transaction, he knew the bank would have to report it, but he wasn't worried — Charles Adderley was going to disappear without a trace, never to be found. With cash bulging in his jacket pockets, he walked two city blocks to a branch of the National Bank, presented his Osker Schmitt documentation, and deposited nine thousand in a newly created account. The bank wouldn't have to report this amount. The teller assured him that his linked debit card could be picked up on Friday.

Five more days in Melbourne would see him out, and he paid Flight Centre cash for a first-class one-way ticket to Bangkok on Royal Thai Airways, departing Monday at 3:35 P.M. He blamed Sonchai for being unable to travel to Paraguay or Brazil directly, but he didn't want those beautiful South American women getting turned off by his love handles. He knew that he could have had liposuction in Melbourne, but as far as he was concerned, Sonchai really was the Da Vinci of plastic surgeons.

When Aspine returned to his apartment, he packed his suitcase, put the keys in an envelope and addressed it to the real estate agent. Once he found out that Mick McHugh and The Executive Suite had his address, he'd had no choice but to leave the apartment. Had Mick asked, he probably would've told him but he didn't like being spied on or having his address on the books of a brothel. He would lose his rent bond of one month's rent but wasn't in the least concerned. *I'm just taking a little insurance. Chin would be proud of me.* After a cursory tidy up, he drove to The Hilton on the Park, on the edge of the city and checked into a suite.

Fifteen minutes later, after unpacking, he drove the hire car into the city and dropped it off, paying the balance owing in cash. When he returned to his room, he destroyed Charles Adderley's passport, driver's license, credit cards and other papers or invoices that bore his name. *Vale Charles Adderley.*

Candy called Muller in the morning and reluctantly agreed to come to his home at 10 P.M. that night. Muller had already teed up one of his former sketch artist mates. The only problem was that he was seventy-five, and there was no way Candy was going believe he was on the force.

Muller sat in his thinking chair looking out at his driveway while telling Bruce Billing to just agree with everything he said. Billing had long flowing white hair, and his skin was brown and wrinkled from the many days he'd spent in his tinnie fishing. It was hard to imagine that he'd ever been a policeman. Headlights swung through the open gates, and Muller grabbed the remote, strode to the garage and closed the roller door. "Thanks for coming, Candy."

"Did I have a choice?"

"Can I get you a drink?"

"Let's get it over with. The longer I'm here, the more nervous I am."

"No one knows you're here. Your name's not in any files, and I'm not even using a police artist. This is Bruce. He's a freelancer who owes me a few favors. When you leave here tonight, he'll erase you from his memory."

"And that'll really take some erasing." Billing laughed as he took a sketch pad from his briefcase. "You're stunning but, yeah, don't worry, I'll forget that I've ever seen you. Besides, this big lug says he'll break my legs if I ever mention you."

"Do we need to do this? Can't I just tell you his name and give you his address? Then you can check him out yourself, and we can forget this sketching bullshit."

"Yeah, but what if he's done a runner. We better get a facial while we can." *Far out. She never said anything about going to his place. I thought he'd gone to the brothel. She's right, but I still want to question her while she's giving Bruce details.*

"He was there a week ago. Why would he have left? Get real."

"Candy, you know what the deal is. You'll be gone and forgotten in less than an hour. Let's get on with it," Muller said sternly. "Tell me about this guy and what makes you think he's behind getting Jack hooked."

She sighed. "He kept asking me if I had been with many young guys. It was creepy. I didn't say much, but as I was leaving, he shouted something about Jack."

"What?"

"It's not important."

"Tell me what he said."

"I told you it's not important," Candy snapped. "I'm out of here."

"Have a look at these noses," Bruce interrupted. "What do you think?"

"Okay, okay, I'm sorry. He mentioned Jack. What else did he say?" Muller asked.

"I was a gift from Mick, and he asked me how well I knew him. He made my skin crawl and got really upset when I called him a John."

"Did he have a large forehead?" Bruce asked.

"No, but it was obvious that he'd had extensive facial surgery. I'd say a full-face lift and crowns or implants. His teeth were just too perfect."

"What color were his eyes?" Muller asked.

"I don't really know. I thought they were black, but you can't have black irises, can you?"

Muller ignored her question. "Did he have any strange mannerisms, you know, eccentricities?"

"When he opened the front door, he was wearing black leather gloves. I was taken aback. He told me that his hands and lower arms had been mangled in a factory accident and he didn't like people seeing them. The scars on his palms and the back of his hands were terrible and it looked like the bottom of his fingers had been sliced off."

"Fingertips?"

"Yeah, they're hard to describe, but the skin looked new and shiny. His hands are ugly, and maybe the surgeon was trying to improve their appearance. If he was, he failed."

Bruce showed his sketch to Candy. "Are we getting close?"

"Yes, but his hair is a darker brown, and his eyes are larger. I suspect he's probably had eye surgery as well. Oh, and his ears are smaller."

Muller looked at the sketch. It was nothing like Aspine. The face he was looking at was thinner, the Grecian nose was gone, the jaw didn't jut, and the full jet-black mane had been replaced with short brown hair. *Is it possible? Perhaps this guy is an intermediary for Aspine, while he's safe and sound, and pulling the strings from an overseas hideaway.*

Bruce made the changes to the sketch and then passed it to Candy. "What do you think?"

"That's him. It's perfect. This has been such a waste of time as you'll see for yourself in the morning, detective. Can you open the roller door? I'm going now."

"Yeah, you've done your part," Muller said, as he walked her to the garage. "Can you think of anything else, birthmarks, moles or tattoos?"

She laughed. "Yes, he had a scar across his lower stomach, obviously a tummy tuck. Anyhow he thinks his plastic surgeon is God but was really annoyed because he hadn't removed his love handles. This guy is incredibly vain. He wouldn't tell me who the surgeon is but he practices in Bangkok and the creep said he was going to see him in the next few weeks for liposuction."

"Thanks, Candy. You've been a big help. I'll be seeing you."

"No, you won't. I never want to lay eyes on you again. Stay away from me," she said, climbing into the Merc.

Bruce was tidying up his crayons when Muller returned. "How'd you like to earn a thousand bucks tomorrow? It might take you one hour, but it could take ten." *Jeez, it's easy spending Raj's money.*

"What do I have to do?"

"Just knock on a door and when it's opened say, 'Are you, Mr. Brown?' I want you to check if the guy matches your sketch."

"I'd love to pick up an easy grand, but why can't you do it?"

"Because it just might be someone who knows me. The sketch looks nothing like the guy I'm thinking of, so I doubt it's him. However, on the off-chance it is, there's no point telegraphing that I'm onto him."

After Bruce had left, Muller scanned the sketch, attached it to a short covering email and sent it to Jasmine, Raj, Fiona, Harry and Sir Edwin.

Chapter 49

IT WAS 8:30 A.M. WHEN Bruce Billing knocked on the front door of the apartment in St Kilda Road. There was no answer, and he took an elevator back down to the foyer and settled in. He cursed, knowing that he wasn't going to pick up a grand for ten minutes work.

Bill Muller had provided his mate on the force with the details of Mary Denton's credit card and bank account. In less than two hours he had called to say he'd located her in a one-bedroom apartment in Richmond. Muller thanked him and asked him to find out all he could about Charles Adderley. Harry was elated when Muller called him with the good news about Mary.

"Thanks, Bill. I'm on my way to beg forgiveness and get her to come back home."

"Good luck, Harry. Did you look at that pic I sent you?"

"Yeah, I've never seen that guy before, and I doubt it's Aspine."

"Yeah. Me too. I know surgeons can perform wonders with plastic surgery, but surely, they can't change every feature. The eyes are different, the nose is different, the ears are different, and the jawline is different."

"Bill, sorry. Can't talk. I have to rush."

"Yeah, you go, Harry, and I sure hope things work out. Keep tonight free though. We're going to have another get-together."

It didn't take long before Muller's contact called to say he had nothing on Charles Adderley and he was getting concerned about the Office of Police Integrity finding out that he was using the force's resources for personal reasons. Muller promised not to ask for any more favors in the near term and hoped that Bruce Billing would have better luck.

He didn't and at 5 P.M. called to report there'd been no sign of life at the apartment all day. He suspected Adderley had done a runner.

The meeting at Jasmine's was somber although everyone was pleased to see Mary with Harry. Raj took the chair at the head of the table and much to Muller's annoyance, assumed control of the meeting. "I've been on the phone all day, and I can you tell that no one named Charles Adderley has left the country in the past week. However, that is not to say that he didn't leave using another name, even though that too is doubtful. I've had the airport's security footage checked, and no one resembling the identikit has boarded an international flight. That said, I'm concerned that the identikit might not be an accurate portrayal, and, if that's the case, this Adderley person might already be in Bangkok. Bill had his apartment staked out today, and it appears that he has vacated."

"That's right," Muller said. "My contact wasn't able to dig anything up on him. I'm going to see the real estate agent in the morning as Adderley had to have provided proof of identification before entering into the lease. With luck, I'll get to see a photocopy of his passport or driver's license."

"You've all looked at the sketch Bill emailed. Are you positive you've never seen this man?" Raj asked.

There were murmured assents before Mary said, "I haven't seen it."

"I haven't seen him, but I've got Craig scanning footage of the audience the night I interviewed William Elmore to see if he can come up with a match," Fiona said.

Muller hastily opened his briefcase and slid the original of the sketch across the table to Mary. "Do you know him?"

"He's familiar," she replied, putting her fingers on her temples. "It's vague, but I'm nearly certain I've seen this man."

"Think," Raj said. "Think."

"Don't pressure her," Harry snapped.

"Be quiet, Harry. You've had me wrapped in cotton wool for the past six months. I can cope with pressure when it's positive."

Mary picked the sketch up and held it close to her face. "I've got it. Harry, don't you remember that fellow admiring our garden? He asked if he could take photos of the shrubs and trees. I said 'yes.' Don't you remember?"

"I-I'm sorry."

"And I'm the one with dementia." Mary laughed. "Think, Harry. He was wearing gloves."

"What?" Muller said.

"Yes. Yes," Harry yelled. "I remember now. I didn't like him. I had a bad feeling about him. I saw him again. I couldn't remember, but he was at the back of the court on the day the shoplifting charge was heard. Please forgive me, Mary."

"Tell me about the gloves," Muller said.

"I thought it was a little strange," Mary said. "It was warm and around midday, yet this fellow was wearing black leather gloves."

"Was he tall?" Muller asked.

"He had a slight hunch, but yes, he was about the same height as Aspine, but nowhere near as heavy," Harry said.

"According to the escort, his hands and lower arms were mangled in a factory accident, and he's very self-conscious. You know what I think? He's had his fingertips removed and his lower arms scarred to make it look like an accident. I think it's Aspine," Muller said. "Sir Edwin, he must've been at the kindergarten the day you were arrested. Are you sure you didn't see him?"

Sir Edwin sighed. "Positive. That image is locked in my mind, and I didn't see that man."

The buzzing of Fiona's cell phone interrupted the meeting, and she answered it in the kitchen. When she returned, she was grim-faced. "According to Craig, he was in the very back row. He has a still of the image that he's trying to define. He'll email us later tonight, and we'll have something better to go on than the sketch."

"What do we do now?" Jasmine asked.

"If he's still here, my little sister, we make sure we put him back in jail. Bill, when you talk to the real estate agent, see if you can get bank details, too."

"Of course," Muller snapped.

It was clear to everyone that Raj was now in charge and calling the shots.

After the meeting broke up, Mary left in her own car. "She's talking to me again, Fiona," Harry said. "But she's staying in her apartment. She said she's not sure whether she wants to live with a man who doesn't trust her. That bastard's ruined my life. As God is my witness, if I knew where he was, I would kill him."

"She'll come back, Harry. She still loves you. Give her time."

Chapter 50

IT WAS FRIDAY, AND in three days' time, Aspine would be on his way to Bangkok. He sat at his desk in the Hilton and looked out across the magnificent parkland, pondering the past six months. He wasn't a killer, but just the thought of killing Jasmine and Raj made him feel warm and fuzzy. It was a strange but satisfying feeling.

He was pleased that he'd managed to conceal his identity and had new legal identification documents. Even more pleasing was that they would know he was the cause of their grief, but have no idea what he looked like. When the time was right, he would return from South America and put Jasmine and Raj through another round of hell. He had hoped that when he left the payback would be complete, but it wasn't. He looked at the notes he had typed and knew that there was a small risk in sending them, but the desire to drive in a few more barbs was overwhelming.

Fiona's note read; *I'm sorry your drunken old man died, bitch, I had a nice bottle of Johnny Walker to give him.*

Harry's read; *Harry, do you remember signing my bonus check for a million bucks? That was satisfying, but not as satisfying as fucking up your marriage.*

Sir Edwin's note read; *When you die, they'll carve Sir Edwin Pedophile on your tombstone.*

Before he knew he was going to jail, Jasmine had said to him on a number of occasions, "I do hope you get everything you so richly deserve." Her note read; *"Jasmine, you got everything you so richly deserve, and there's more to come. Give Jack my best.*

Raj's note read; *"You'll still have money and power, but the prestige and status you crave has gone forever."*

Aspine bought a cheap hoodie in the city, and despite the heat, put it on and pulled the hood over his head. Ten minutes later still wearing the hoodie and having added sunglasses, he entered the office of a small courier, carrying five envelopes. "I want each of these delivered at exactly 4 P.M. on Monday."

"We'll have to use five couriers, sir. That will be expensive. If–"

Aspine cut the young sales assistant off. "I know. I'm not worried. Now listen to me. They have to be delivered at 4 P.M. If the recipients aren't home, you can leave them in their mailboxes. Is that clear?"

"Yes, yes, I understand."

Aspine paid cash and nonchalantly strolled through the gardens on the way back to the Hilton. *I'd love to see their faces when they open those envelopes.*

Bill Muller knew he was treading on dangerous ground when he flashed his wallet at the real estate agent and started questioning him. Luckily the agent didn't ask to check his identification and a few minutes later told him that Charles Adderley had sent the keys back, had vacated the apartment, had not claimed his bond money and had not left a forwarding address. When Muller asked about bank details, they were provided with surprising alacrity. The copy of Adderley's passport was black and white and of poor quality, but it matched the sketch. Muller's ploy of wearing an open suit coat which allowed glimpses of his shoulder holster was paying dividends.

Muller rationalized that he'd been lucky with Candy and the real estate agent but impersonating a policeman was a serious offense. He was unlikely to be able to fool a branch manager of the Commonwealth Bank. He called his mate on the force and begged him to check out the bank details, promising him that he wouldn't ask any more favors. Thirty minutes later Muller felt sick when told that Adderley had cleared the balance and closed his bank account two days earlier.

We're too late. He's flown the coop.

When Muller called Raj and told him, he was sure Aspine was already out of the country, the Singaporean became angry.

"He can't be. I told you there has been no sign of him in international departures on the security footage over the past seven days. He's still here."

"I don't think so," Muller responded. "He's been one step ahead of us all the way. What if he took a domestic flight to Sydney or drove there and then hopped it to Bangkok? That's if he's really going there? It wouldn't surprise me if he's halfway to South America as we speak."

Raj paused. "Yes, you may be right, but my gut says you're not. I'll get Sydney international departures checked out."

"It doesn't have to be Sydney. It could be any of our international airports," Muller sighed in exasperation.

"Keep looking, Bill. I just know he hasn't left."

Chapter 51

THAI AIRWAYS FLIGHT TG466 departed Melbourne precisely on time at 3:35 P.M. bound for Bangkok without stopovers. Douglas Aspine relaxed in a luxurious first-class cabin sipping Jack Daniels. He closed his eyes and pondered the past year and how clever he had been. His future lay in South America, and he was looking forward to sampling the beautiful señoritas. If only Sonchai had removed his love handles he'd be on his way there now. He had spent far more money escaping and pursuing vengeance than he'd ever anticipated, but still had nearly ten mil in the Caymans — enough to live a very comfortable life in Argentina, Brazil or Paraguay. *I might even buy a business and export merchandise to Australia. Labor is cheap, and regulations are loose. I might be able to make some serious money.* He checked his watch and smiled. It was 4 P.M. The losers would be opening their envelopes. A flight attendant asked if she could do anything for him and he ordered another Jack Daniels. *Life is good.*

Jasmine opened her envelope and said, "He has a very long memory."

"The fool has gone, but he had to have one final word," Raj replied, reading his note. "I have to make a few calls. Jasmine, call Bill Muller and ask him to come here. Then call the others and get them to come too. I'm sure they will also have notes."

By 7 P.M. Raj was seated at the head of Jasmine's dining table relating what he knew to the others. "He's on a Thai Airways flight to Bangkok traveling under the name of Osker Schmitt. It departed nearly four hours ago."

"How do you know?" Muller asked.

"They matched his photo going through international departures, and then it was just a matter of time before they found out what airline and flight he was on."

"It's a pity they didn't find out before he boarded. It's too late to do anything now," Muller said.

"Good riddance," Jasmine said.

"He's gotten away," Harry growled. "I would've loved to have seen him back in Changi."

"Me, too," Sir Edwin said.

"I'm like Jasmine," Fiona said. "I'm just glad we've seen the last of him."

"I know hate chews you up," Harry said. "All of my life I've tried to turn the other cheek and take the positives out of life. This man ruined my company and nearly destroyed my marriage. I'm sorry. I hate him so badly. I feel physically sick."

"I guess there's no point hanging around," Muller said, standing. "The ladies are right. There's nothing we can do now, and all hate will do is destroy us. Let's not wait another ten years before we catch up again."

"Don't go, Bill. Stay around for a cup of coffee or tea. Besides, I still have to settle up with you," Raj said. "This wasn't your fight but the contribution you made and the hours you put in were outstanding."

"Hear, hear," Fiona said.

"Well done, Bill," Sir Edwin said, patting him on the back.

"Thank you, Raj. I'm surprised you're taking it so well. You were so determined to put him back behind bars," Muller said.

Raj's cell phone rang, and he excused himself to take the call in the kitchen. They could hear him talking in Malay, and while Jasmine picked up a few words, she didn't get the gist of the conversation. When he returned half an hour later, he said, "I'm sorry. Business never rests."

"I feel flat, washed out." Sir Edwin moaned. "He really did a job on us. The bastard."

"We would've all preferred a different outcome, but sitting around moping isn't going to change anything," Fiona said.

Jasmine served the tea and coffee with an enticing chocolate cake, but the mood of the room didn't lift. The rich aroma of the coffee failed to block out the stench of defeat. Raj's cell phone rang again, and he excused himself. This time he spoke in the distinctly sing-song Thai language, and no one could understand a word. The conversation was long, and while they couldn't understand it, Raj's voice progressively became more demanding.

"He speaks five languages," Jasmine said, almost apologetically.

When he came back to the table, Fiona asked, "More business?"

"Not really." Raj laughed. "I have some good news."

Aspine had consumed at least ten whiskeys and converted his seat to a bed. He was sound asleep when a flight attendant entered his cabin. She picked up two glasses being careful not to touch the rims and placed them in a plastic bag. Thirty minutes later, she returned and gently shook him. "Wake up, sir. We're landing in fifteen minutes."

His head was heavy, and he was drowsy, but when he looked at his watch, he knew they'd only been in the air for eight hours. "I don't understand. How can we have made such good time?"

"Oh, you must have slept through the captain's announcement. We've been flying into heavy headwinds, and we're making a short stopover to refuel."

"Where?"

"Singapore, sir."

Aspine started shaking uncontrollably. "God no," he said.

"Don't worry, sir. Everyone will remain on the plane, and we'll be underway again very quickly. The captain will do his best to make up time. Please fasten your seatbelt."

Aspine groaned. *Why didn't I go to South America? I feel sick. Perhaps I'm overreacting, and the plane really does have to be refueled. Yes, that's it. How would anyone know I'm on the plane or have the power to divert it?*

Sir Edwin's mouth was agape. "You have enough influence to do that?"

"Raj, I love you," Fiona said. "I'd kill to be at Singapore airport when that plane lands.'

"Don't worry. You'll get to see him being marched off the plane in handcuffs," Raj said. "The media will be there in force."

"But how did you do it?" Harry said, shaking his head.

"I didn't do anything." Raj smiled grimly. "I just told those in power in the Singapore government that the escapee, Douglas Aspine, was traveling on a Thai Airways flight to Bangkok, under the name Osker Schmitt. You have to realize his escape made fools of many powerful people and saving face in Singapore is very important. The Thai and Singapore militaries have had a very close relationship for nearly thirty years and have been partners in maintaining regional security. Singapore's done a lot of favors for Thailand including donating seven second-hand F-16s to it in 2004. This is an opportunity for Thailand to repay a favor."

"We heard you talking in Thai. What was that about?" Fiona asked.

"I have some very large investments in Thailand and the minister for industry is a good friend. I asked him to use his influence to persuade those who may not want to help. That's all."

"You shouted at him," Fiona said.

Raj laughed. "You misheard. I would never be so disrespectful."

Bill Muller hadn't said a word. "How are the police in Singapore going to prove it's him? You said they don't have his DNA and if I'm right, he no longer has any fingerprints. And we all know that the man on the plane looks nothing like the Douglas Aspine of ten years ago."

"When he divorced Barbara, he cheated her out of what was rightfully hers. She has been living a hard life with few of the luxuries she once enjoyed," Raj said.

"We all know that, Raj, but what's that got to do with identifying him?" Muller said.

"She has three children, the youngest, Mark, is eighteen and still living at home. He's the same age as Jack. Jasmine and I visited her the day after Mary recognized the man in the sketch. We knew we had to find a way to identify him. We told Barbara what we thought Aspine had done to Jack. She was appalled."

"She is a lovely woman," Jasmine interrupted. "We asked her if Mark might be willing to provide his DNA, and she said she could do better than that. She asked us to follow her into the laundry which we thought was a little strange. Then she sifted through the dirty laundry until she came across a blood-stained yellow and blue singlet. Mark plays basketball, and he'd copped a knock to his nose at the weekend."

"She gave you the singlet," Fiona said.

"Yes and no," Jasmine smiled. "Raj felt very sorry for her and agreed to buy it for–"

"That's unimportant," Raj cut in. "What's important is that the police will now be able to prove it's him." *Five hundred thousand is not a large amount for me, and it will make Barbara's life a lot easier. I would have paid ten times more for that singlet.*

"Where is the singlet?" Muller asked.

"It will be in Singapore in the morning."

"What a fool he turned out to be," Sir Edwin said.

"No, he was not a fool," Raj said. "He was as cunning as a fox, but he was loose-lipped, vain and arrogant too. That's what brought him down. If he hadn't mentioned Bangkok to the girl, if he hadn't wanted more plastic surgery and if he hadn't sent us those notes, he'd still be free."

The front page of *The Straits Times* carried a large photo of Douglas Aspine being hauled off the Thai Airways jet in handcuffs under the headline, *Escapee Recaptured.* There were two smaller before and after facial photos below it. Police said the apprehended escapee continued to deny he was Douglas Aspine but they were in no doubt, and DNA evidence would soon confirm their assertions. The attorney general said the recapture was the result of six months of painstaking police work and the community could feel proud of their police force.

Douglas Aspine sat in one of the cells in Changi Police Station, head between his legs, racking his brain trying to fathom where he had slipped up. His face was stark white, his eyes were bloodshot, and his head pounded from the whiskeys. He had asked to see a lawyer. When the police had suggested Teo Boon Wan, the lawyer who had defended him ten years earlier, Aspine had denied knowing him. He was still not without hope because even if they forced him to give a saliva or blood sample, they had nothing to match his DNA with. *If I get a good lawyer, I'll walk away from this. They'll never prove I'm Douglas Aspine.*

Aspine woke to see the inspector, who had interrogated him the night before smiling at the small barred window in the cell door. "Good morning, Mr. Aspine."

"I told you that's not my name. You have the wrong man. I'm Osker Schmitt."

"I believe your son, Mark, is a very good basketball player."

"I don't have a son. I have no family."

The inspector ignored what Aspine had said. "When he was playing last weekend, he took a solid knock to his nose, and it bled all over his singlet."

"What's that got to do with me?"

The inspector smiled. "We have his singlet, and you know what else we have. The glasses you drank from on the plane. You're going to die in Changi prison, Mr. Aspine."

Aspine took a few seconds to absorb the inspector's words, and then he let out a harrowing scream, "No, no," and fell on the floor sobbing.

Reviews:
Good, bad or indifferent are important for readers and authors alike. The Amazon links are:

U.S. http://a.co/bO3FqKb
U.K. http://amzn.eu/7n88WNS
Canada http://a.co/d8EvLmU
India http://amzn.in/j8XL1AI

Other Books By Peter Ralph

More white collar crime suspense thrillers by Peter Ralph are on the drawing board.

For updates about new releases, as well as exclusive promotions, visit the author's website and sign up for the VIP mailing list at http://www.peterralphbooks.com/

Visit here to get started:
Amazon USA: http://goo.gl/Ya6GB7
Amazon UK: http://goo.gl/Uxc4ly

FREE DOWNLOAD

FOG CITY FRAUD

Why is an irate investor holding his advisor's receptionist hostage on the 16th level of a high rise building?
Sign up for Peter Ralph's reader's group and get your free copy of the novella Fog City Fraud: a financial suspense thriller.

Visit here to get started:
http://www.peterralphbooks.com/

www.ingramcontent.com/pod-product-compliance
Lightning Source LLC
Chambersburg PA
CBHW021146130626
46554CB00005B/1685